Dancing
to Raven's Song

a novel

Michael R. Patton

Myth^Steps Productions
Peace Mill Publishing

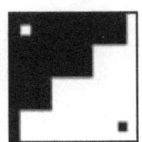

ISBN 978-1-953996-12-1

author's note:

This work was original published in softcover, in 1999, under the title *The Raven's Way*. So if you bought that book, I guess you don't really need to buy this book. After all, I've made no major changes. However, I did make around 5,000 minor changes. Literally.

To be honest, I don't think I made those changes for you, dear reader. No, I seem to be driven by a curse placed upon me in childhood: the curse of wanting to get something right. I don't know that this edition is "right", but I do know it's better.

about the author:

Michael R. Patton, in his own words, "likes to make stuff". This stuff includes novels, new fables and myths, poetry, cartoons, essays, and videos. The ideas that run through that work can be found in the titles of his books. For example: "Searching for My Best Beliefs". Basically self-taught, he describes his slow, tedious journey of discovery as "crawling blindfolded through the labyrinth". He has lived and worked all over the United States.

THE CREATION STORY

*"So, you're convinced you must become a shaman?"
I said to her. "Well, okay, I'll teach you—teach you how
to find what you already know—what you know, deep
within."*

In the very time that I waited to die, a young raven
new to the flock had come to me for instruction. But
how could I possibly focus on her, filled as I was by the
tension of uncertainty? At odd moments, I can feel
that other world beckoning (perhaps "threatening" is
the better word), filling my frame with a hurried,
excited vibration. But then, just as abruptly, the feeling
will pass. Life then becomes mundane again. I am not
yet done.

While awaiting my decision, the young bird had
paced about, scraping her tail feathers through the dust
outside my cave, looking up at the tall redwoods with
lost eyes.

I could see the path of her travels had spun her in
mad spirals. The clear simple line had soon grown
tangled and painful. But she'd found a way through
that wild labyrinth and at the end, landed here, at my
cave. She knew she was not here by chance: she knew
she was to become a shaman. A job she'd once rejected.
I understood—I'd felt that same reluctance at first.

But before instruction could commence, I needed
to remind her of our lineage, of how we all descended
from Raven. "We must never forget: Raven is within
us," I told the neophyte. "Though we are common
ravens, we are also Raven.

"As you know, Raven was here from the beginning, the very beginning. But the idea for the world did not come from Raven, but from the he and she known as the Creator. In order to make this idea real, the Creator took some mud and took some water and put Raven together."

The Creator then set Raven down and gave him a spin. As Raven revolved, his vision blurred; what he had once seen as one, he now saw as many. And when Raven came to rest again, all the things he had seen surrounded him. Yes, there were birds: coots, eagles, owls, sparrows, hummingbirds, pelicans, vultures, and many more—more birds than there were stars in heaven. And yes, there were other creatures too: snakes, whales, flies, mice, geese, moose, and mongoose, to name just a few. Raven saw all of them, but saw none as either good or bad—when his vision had blurred, good and bad had combined. So, though man may attempt to distinguish between the two, Raven never even tries.

Yes, I know Coyote often takes credit for the creation of our world, citing stories of dubious origin. What a poor deluded creature! How does he expect anyone to believe him?—that such a mangy, low-slung, lice-infested creature could be capable of creating something so grand!

Coyote has fooled no one but himself. Everyone knows that after the creatures were created, Raven made the earth, the mountains, the water, the sky for them. Consider this: the world was created out of darkness. Even light came from darkness. And what is darker than Raven?

Yes, vultures are black and crows are black, but Raven is even blacker—the essence of darkness, the essence of mystery, and therefore, the essence of the Universe.

I waited, allowing all this to sink in. But the neophyte just stared at me with blank black eyes. I realized what she wanted—she wanted to know how I'd become what she would become. But I did not wish to go through that story, my story, again: even with the perspective of time and understanding, I still feel the pain.

Yet I knew that I needed share that story again. Share what I'd learned—gained—in my early days. Though in so doing, I must also share the pain.

Part I

My first year on this earth was relatively easy. The water ran freely through my fledgling summer. The winter did not shiver my bones.

But I felt at odds with my family. My interests did not mesh with those of my three siblings. While their ambitions were of a mundane sort, I dreamed of leaving our desert in search of the mountains and the sea. I wanted to strip off the shackles of family and flock and be that lone raven seen black against a white cloud, inspiring awe in all who see it.

My grandfather had fathered many broods and knew how to care for his families' physical needs. But he had never challenged the larger questions of life; he had never looked within.

And though my father was hungry to explore life's mysteries, the practicalities of daily living kept him anchored. As a result, he was never quite here nor there and often had a hard time putting his thoughts together. Since my sister and two brothers did not share my desire for knowledge, Father's behavior did not bother them. But I had questions. I wanted to know how the spirit-self of a crow differed from that of a raven. Why did my mood always change with the setting of the sun? And where exactly was The Realm of the One-In-All?

Only once did my father speak to me of The Realm, the place that is the home source of Raven, the place where all the knowledge of Raven is kept.

On that particular day, Father and I had been out hunting when we paused under the ledge of a bluff.

Everything was still and breathless with the summer heat. The desert plain lay flat and white under a merciless sun. Without looking at me, my father said, "So, the shaman tells me you have already visited The Realm."

"Yes, I have," I admitted. "But my experiences haven't been so clear. More like a feeling, an impression, a dream of knowing."

"Experiences? You've been more than once?"

"Three times."

That made him jump. "Can you go there at will?"

"Yeah, I guess so. The first time, I wasn't even trying. 'Summoned,' that's the word, right? An odd experience. I talked to the shaman and he told me of a way to create the experience for myself. But I've only tried it twice."

"He told you of a way? You're the only one I know who's been told of a way. I've been summoned a couple of times in my life. Just like most. It comes upon us and we must go. What'd you do there?"

"I thought we weren't supposed to talk of such things."

"Well, no, generally speaking. Not in detail anyway. You didn't encounter the Master Raven, did you?"

"No, no, but I did meet a guide."

"Everyone does. Okay, well, that's enough. But I'm wondering...maybe the shaman believes you're destined to follow him."

That put me on my tail feathers. Me, a shaman? No way. Though I yearned for knowledge, I did not wish to torture myself, to submit myself to the rigorous, painful practices of shamanic training. I was not yet a full-grown adult and would likely pass another year before mating. I was looking forward to enjoying a free season, a season without responsibility. Then maybe—maybe—I would settle down. But not as a shaman. Not with that burden weighing me down.

Without waiting for an answer, Father continued. "I know I haven't helped you much. That is, beyond practical matters. At one time, I actually wished to become a shaman myself. But my capacity did not match my desire. Roe, your mind spans wide— you're driven to seek without you knowing what it is you seek. This urge is both a blessing and a curse. But you're too young to realize that. So what are your plans?"

"I don't know for sure," I said. "I only know that I don't want to become a shaman. Not now, not later, not ever."

I thought again of our old shaman. Just visiting him made my pin feathers stand on end. He was the soul of our flock, or so we believed. None of the birds dared speak against him. We believed he knew everything. Through him the flock communed with the Master Raven.

"Besides," I continued, "how could I ever become a shaman? No one in our family has ever been a shaman."

My father scratched a rock with his claw. "Sometimes you are born into something, other times you get to choose, then other times the thing chooses you."

"I think I would have known by now," I said.

He looked directly at me then. In that look were many things, things which I could not yet decipher. Years later, I wonder if I did not underestimate my father.

In the next moment, Father spread his wings and dove off the ledge. I followed his lead and plunged back into the dry, airless heat.

My mother tended to her brood with a dull simplicity; she had an impartial kindness that made her seem both caring and remote. Though I would have appreciated more attention, at the same time, I enjoyed being left to my own resources. This freedom helped me develop self-reliance—but also made me seem just a little aloof.

I guess you could say my upbringing gave me an ambivalent attitude toward life. But this ambivalence had one key benefit: I could see the upside of any situation, as well as its downside; I gained perspective. And though this perspective added to my aloofness, it also gave me a sense of empathy. I could see my fellow ravens better from a distance. The trouble was, I often had difficulty seeing myself. And for that reason, I had to suffer the long trail before I arrived at my final destination.

Whatever resources I had built up were sorely tested in my second summer when a drought came and scorched the life from the land. Our creek dried up; the naked earth cracked for want of water. Our flock had no other choice but to leave its roosting place and scour the desert en masse, hunting for food and fresh water. But the farther we went, the less we found.

Eventually, our path collided with that of three other raven flocks, coming at us from three different directions. Like us, they searched the desert for basics. Like us, they were going mad with frustration.

All four flocks realized the futility of their course and decided to rest. Our flock found a ring of boulders on the flat plain and settled down to roost.

We had a ruling council of five elders. These elder birds could see that we were in a no-win situation. So they put forth a plan whereby they could protect their authority.

They went to the elders of the other three flocks and suggested a meeting that would determine our collective fate. Each flock would elect one representative to be sent to the meeting.

The others readily agreed to this idea. No elder would be eligible for nomination—freeing them from responsibility. Like our own elders, they realized any decision that came from this meeting would likely be unpopular—perhaps very unpopular.

Our flock contained twelve broods. Each brood was asked to put forth a nominee to voted on by the entire flock.

The council elders went from brood to brood, gathering the names of the candidates. At the end, they approached my family.

An old bird with a stooped neck hopped forward to address us. "For generations, we've held the belief that a certain obscure individual would be called upon, in a time of crisis, to lead us," he said. "We also believe that until the moment of crisis, no one would be aware of that bird's role, including the chosen bird its own self.

"We of the elder council feel that now is the time for this leader to emerge. Will he or she come from your own strong family? We must find out! You must put forth one of your own as a nominee."

My father turned to me. I knew he believed that I might be that bird of destiny.

What could I do, but agree to represent our brood. What did I have to fear? Eleven other birds had also answered the call, and all were either better physical specimens or from families larger or more popular than my own. My chances for election were slim indeed.

The following day, the electorate gathered in a clearing encircled by twelve scrawny trees—a tree for each candidate. I chose my tree, flew down to a low branch, and waited.

As a nominee was introduced, all those who

supported this bird would fly to his or her tree. The candidate with the most birds on his branches at the end would be the flock's representative. My name was last on the list.

As expected, each nominee received the support of its own brood and a few other birds—usually those who didn't care much for their own kin. By the time they announced my name, only a couple outside my family had failed to commit.

But at that moment, I was blessed—or rather, cursed—by an unexpected event: a cloud of locust suddenly materialized above my tree. Churning angrily with their nasal hum, they descended straight down into its branches and leaves.

Ravens shot like black arrows at the tree, creating a spangled mix of sunlight and green as they pierced through the leaves. A flickering, a flashing of black wings. The birds nabbed the bugs in mid-air, choked them down while still in flight, then dove down to feast some more. I froze, afraid to move.

In moments, the din abruptly stilled. Not a locust in sight. The majority of the flock now roosted in my tree. The limbs sagged with their black bodies. My new-found friends lifted their beaks and cawed in praise of me.

To my confusion and surprise, I had won by a landslide.

Immediately following the election, the council elders surrounded me and led me to a nearby cave. I expected them to impart some special knowledge that would help me perform my duty. But no—they merely said: "Well, it's all up to you now. Tomorrow, at midday, you will meet with the representatives of the other three flocks."

"What should I do in the meantime?" I asked,

feeling a bit bewildered. "I mean, how will I know what to do or say at the meeting? How will I know what decision to make? Maybe I should talk with the shaman. What do you think?"

The elders looked at one another. They didn't trust what the shaman might say. But how could they refuse me?

"Yeah, that'd probably be okay," the stooped-neck elder said. "Go ahead and see the shaman."

But they insisted on flying with me to the nook in a cliff where the shaman now roosted. They then perched in a nearby tree to keep an eye on me.

Since the shaman's answers came from the Master Raven, we believed they always contained truth and wisdom—though sometimes you really had to look for those qualities. Any message I received from him would be respected by the entire flock. But wise old bird that he was, he kept away from politics. During times of stress, he always advised patience and fortitude, reminding us all that hardship is a test, that a life without pain is no real blessing.

"The difficulties of life wake us up to ourselves," the shaman told us time after time. "As an individual pulls more from his depths, he adds to himself, and to the flock, and also to The Realm of the One-In-All, because The Realm contains the sum of all we have been. The Realm holds the idea of Raven, the essence of Raven energy—a distillation. Through our growth, we each add to that energy—a power Raven uses in its role as caretaker of this world and all the world's creatures— including man. Without the power of our energy to sustain it, the Earth would slowly go into decline 'til it was nothing more than a dead clump hanging in space."

Yes, that's what he told us to believe.

As I stood before the shaman at the entrance to his

little cave, I felt the lift of confidence. I had been chosen; I was special—my election had clearly been the will of the Master Raven.

"Have you prepared yourself for this sacrifice?" the old shaman asked in a deep croaking voice.

What did he mean "sacrifice"? "I have been selected," I said proudly. "It was just like a miracle."

"A miracle? No, no, not a miracle. The Master Raven chose you because you needed this experience."

"What? Why?"

"That I can not tell you. You will learn in time. If I told you now, you would not understand."

"So any ideas about tomorrow? Any suggestions about what I should say, what I should do?"

"Trust yourself."

How frustrating! I wanted more information. "But what's going to happen?"

"You will survive."

That put me on my tail feathers. Despite all the hardships of the drought, I had not confronted the possibility of my own death until that moment.

"I said you would survive, so now you worry about death." The old shaman shook his head. "Up to this point, your life experience has been relatively mild. But that curse has just ended. Accept this great responsibility, this terrible burden, and be off! Get a good rest—you have much ahead of you."

He raised his long wings, creating a shroud above me. I dared not question him more. I left the cliff and, with shaky wing, flew back to the circle of boulders. The elders followed right behind me.

The council elders quarantined me that evening in a niche under a large rock. I was allowed only a brief visit with my family. To my surprise, Grandfather and Mother and Father cawed with pride as they

14

surrounded me. I'd never received such praise from them. On the other hand, my sister and two brothers stood in the background, uncertain what to think of their sibling.

I awoke the next morning wobbled and bleary after a restless night's sleep. While the sun crept upward on its arc, I waited impatiently. Thoughts swarmed in my head, refusing to be calmed. Finally, the elders came for me. I followed them to a small clearing at the bottom of a dark hollow. When they had gone, I paced about, scraping my feet through the small dry leaves.

In short order, three young birds, representatives from the other flocks, dropped down into the hollow.

No one knew what to say. We just stood there, looking at one another awkwardly, secretly judging.

I was the youngest, but none of us were full-grown. I introduced myself. The others followed. Bok, the bird closest to me, shifted his weight from foot to foot. He kept his head low and his eyes hooded, which made him seem shy and wary. Standing to the other side, Mor and Prok both appeared self-assured, cool and thoughtful. Strangely enough, they did not once exchange glances.

"Well," I said, "here we are. Anyone have any idea about what to do? How to proceed?"

"My elder council just told me to do my best," Mor said.

"Mine didn't give me much either," Prok said. "All I know is, we must reach a decision today."

I felt I needed to assert myself, otherwise Mor and Prok might own the meeting. Their confidence worried me. So I took a breath, puffed up my chest and said, "Let us first state the problem. We have no food. At least, not enough for all four flocks. And very little water. There's drought everywhere you turn. So, if there's not enough for everyone, some must, well, sacrifice, I guess."

"Okay, we have defined the problem," Prok said. "Too many birds, not enough resources. Obviously, we can't magically create more of what we need, so then, we must dispense with some of the birds."

"But which birds do we dispense with?" Mor said. "The elderly, the hobbled, the wing-sore?"

"No, that would still leave too many birds," Prok said, taking two paces to one side, then two to the other.

"What are you suggesting?" I asked. "Voluntary suicide?"

"No," Prok said, looking at me with dull solemn eyes, "I have a better idea. My proposal would allow birds to die with dignity. Plus, the survivors would be the strongest birds, the ones most likely to withstand the famine. If we allowed suicide, only the bravest would give up their lives. The ravens of our flocks must win the right to survive. They must fight for their lives. We say—that is, *I* say we hold a battle. Flock against flock, one against all. The idea shocks you, I'm sure, but wait before you protest—we will exempt fledglings and young mothers. Think about it and then tell me, is this plan not reasonable and just?"

I did not hesitate but immediately spoke my outrage. "Raven killing raven? That's your solution? In order to save our lives, we must degrade ourselves? As the shaman always says, everything we do contributes to who we are. It's not just our physical survival at stake here, but our emotional and spiritual life as well; our dignity, our integrity. What we do here will actually affect all ravens, now and in the future."

Mor and Prok raked their talons through the leaves. Bok looked at them, then at me, then at them, then at me.

"You speak well," Mor said. "But your words don't

16

put food in the mouths of my loved ones. I have to worry about their survival right now, at this moment, *in this realm*. We're supposed to contribute to the lineage of Raven by starving to death?"

Before I could think to answer, Mor turned to Bok and said, "How about you? You have any enlightening thoughts on the subject?"

Bok shifted from foot to foot and shook his wings. "Well, yes, no. I mean, I don't know. There are so many things to consider. No matter what we do, some will die. I don't know...life and death. Shamans. Starvation. You see, last spring, my sister fell ill. So Father went to the shaman for help. The old bird came to our roost and did his routine. But still, my sister died the next morning. Nothing to be done about it." He hung his head, sunk in the memory.

Mor and Prok just stood there, nodding at him.

Though I sympathized, I wondered how this bird had ever gotten himself elected. Obviously, after the death of his sister, he had stopped caring about what happened in this world, this physical realm. I could see that whatever his misgivings might be, he would agree to Mor and Prok's plan eventually, giving them a majority.

But I was not done yet.

"I say we allow some birds to sacrifice themselves first," I said. "But not the young and not adults of a certain age. After that, we can consider your plan again. Perhaps by that time we will have come up with some alternatives."

"We cannot wait for alternatives," Prok shouted. "There are no alternatives. Your hesitancy only prolongs our suffering. As I said, if we allowed any suicide, the noblest would die for the sake of cowards. That isn't right. Let us vote now. How many in favor of staging a battle between the four flocks?"

I spread my wings out in frustration, then looked over to Bok. He leaned forward and nudged a pebble with his beak. "Come on!" I cawed at him. "Listen to your heart. To destroy one another this way, can that be right?"

"But Roe, you know that we will all enjoy many other lifetimes in this earth realm," Prok cut in. "After this one, another will follow, then another and so on. So then, what's the problem with staging a battle?"

Bok seemed relieving by this line of reasoning.

"I know you have experienced loss," I said to him, "but that doesn't mean you have to surrender your will. I can see that you know their idea is wrong. Do we simply drop our ideals in difficult times? I have experienced The Realm. I know the power of its reality. Mor and Prok are asking us to ignore the truth told by our shamans. If you vote with me, it will be a stalemate. Then we'll be forced to consider alternatives or else take the vote to the flocks. You find it so impossible to resist them? All you have to say is 'no'."

"Birds starve as we bicker here," said Mor.

"Save your flock!" Prok cawed.

"I'm sorry," Bok said to me. "But I don't want to argue here all day. I just don't have it in me. There's no other way out really. So let's be done with it."

Though I continued to plead my case, I could feel the moment slipping away.

"You have refused your strength," I told Bok, "because to own it, you would have to go beyond your pain." For the first time in my life, I really wanted something—something beyond my personal desires, beyond my selfish dreams. But I was blind to how my words wounded Bok and moved him farther away from me.

Mor and Prok waited patiently until Bok and I had finished our little drama. They knew he was too weak to make a stand and that I did not know how to manipulate him. When we finally took a vote, the count was three to one.

As I flew from the hollow, my wings felt leaden. I wobbled through the air, listing from one side to the other.

When I told the council elders the verdict, to my surprise, they did not protest, but suggested I deliver the news to the flock myself. Though they followed me back to the clearing, they made sure they kept their distance.

Birds were huddled in the shadowy nooks of the boulders, trying to escape the afternoon heat. I fluttered down to the center of the clearing. The wind lifted me just as my feet touched ground and threw me back on my tail—an embarrassing landing, adding to the humiliation I already felt.

The broods left the shadows and gathered around me. Though weakness filled my bones, I realized that, for the moment at least, I was the flock's leader. On my way here, I had rehearsed a speech in my head. But now all those words, so carefully chosen, seemed completely false.

To the side, I could see the members of my family, attempting, as usual, to remain inconspicuous. But at the same time, they held their heads up with pride. How would they feel after they heard the results of the meeting?

I took a breath and surveyed the whole flock. There was no way out but to tell it.

"It has been decided," I began. "We decided, or rather, they decided, because, though I don't deny my responsibility, I did argue against this plan, loud and long I fought, but you see, I was only one vote against three, so what could I do?" "Just tell us the decision," someone cried.

I felt so young now, a fledgling weak of wing. "The other three representatives, believing that we must thin our ranks in order to survive, voted to hold a battle, a fight involving all four flocks, one against all."

The roar of their protest hit me in a wave. I spoke quickly, attempting to push my voice above the tumult. "I tried to reason with them," I yelled. "But their flocks are starving. Fledglings and old ones are dying. They said this way the strongest will survive, the ones capable of enduring the famine. They rejected my pleas. Yeah, you make noise now, but who among you came to me with a plan I could offer to them?"

Fortunately, my shabby excuses were lost in all the ruckus. I knew that, for the time being, I could do nothing else but accept their abuse. So I tried to breathe evenly and remain calm, telling myself that the flock would soon quiet down—their wild cries could not last forever.

But no, that's not true: even now, I see and hear that huddled mob—their breaks lifted high, emitting shrieks of pain and horror.

"Coward!" one bird cawed.

"Fool!" another screamed.

"We'd be better off starving to death."

Considering this response, you may wonder why they didn't try to avoid this fight by taking flight. Maybe they did consider that option, but saw that it solved one problem, without solving the other. However, I like to think: we believed in remaining true to agreements made.

But I also think: we did as we did because this event had a will of its own. In other words: what happened happened the way it was supposed to happen. Yes, that's what I believe. And yet, I still feel some guilt over what occurred—as well I should. A belief in destiny should not free me from responsibility.

When the protest had quieted a bit, a big bird strutted up to me. He jumped onto a rock, looked down his black beak at me, and shook his head. Roc was his name. He took great pleasure in criticism. When nothing more could be done, when nothing could be changed, that's when you heard him speak. Though the flock usually ignored his harsh judgments, they now settled down to listen.

"So what made an empty-headed tyro like you think you could handle those birds of experience?" he began.

"Three against one," I protested. "Three against one!"

"Shut up! Shut up before you cause more trouble!"

Roc then launched an attack heard by all and cheered by most. I knew I was being unjustly blamed, yet his words struck me to the core. I couldn't help but feel that I'd jeopardized the fate of the entire flock. Many would die as a result of my failure.

"So, when is this war of yours?" Roc asked, in conclusion.

"Tomorrow, mid-morning, in the clearing of the twelve trees."

Again, the flock exploded with wild wailing cries. But I continued, just wanting to get done with it.

"When the call is given, all four flocks will converge in the center of the clearing. Each one battling the other three—one against all, as I said. We agreed to abide by certain rules. The youngest can remain behind. Expectant mothers. The elderly need not participate, unless they so choose. But those capable of defending themselves must—or else face expulsion from their flock."

Roc made a derisive cry, fanned his tail feather at me, then flew off. Still moaning and crying, the broods began to disperse. When most had cleared away, I hobbled off, relieved to be alone.

I thought my family might shun me. But to my surprise, they gathered around and stroked my wings in a display of affection quite unlike them. I could only manage to say a choked "thanks".

"No, son, we thank you," my father said. "I have never been so proud." This praise came from a raven who'd barely acknowledged the first time I took wing.

But soon, the old awkwardness overcame better impulse. So we shuffled off to our nook under the boulder for the evening. Each then nestled down into his or her own private thoughts and dreams.

The night brought a drizzly rain, teasing us with moisture that quickly disappeared into the sandy soil. Perhaps it was the dampness, but my young limbs creaked like those of an old codger.

I sensed that my brothers, Kol and Ral, were excited by the thought of doing battle—eager to prove themselves brave.   I wondered how could I bridge the distance between us. My heart felt so weak now; I didn't have the energy to try.

Why had I been born into this family? A basic indefinable difference blocked any true closeness. And yet I still felt a bond.

Even my sister, Ka'a, had to go into the field. She'd never killed more than a grubworm. Fear and confusion roiled within her—I could feel her uncertainty. This event was beyond her imagining. She could not accept what was happening. She'd been told that her life goal was to find a mate and raise a brood. Now she felt the pain of one deceived.

The passing shower had freshened the air, so the next morning felt a little like spring. Sunlight glistened on the rocks and a few small yellow flowers had sprung from the ground.

The council elders came to me at daybreak and said I should lead the flock into battle.

They waited until the others had roused themselves, then signaled to me. Afraid to hesitate, I took flight.

Upon arriving at the clearing of twelve trees, we found the other three flocks already perched and prepared for war. What a commotion of shrieks and caws and fluttering and rustling of wings! I led the flock to the trees along the north side, then settled down on a branch with my family and waited. I exchanged one brief look with Grandfather and Father and Mother—a look of love but not of warmth; a look that said: "So here we are." To say a "farewell" would be to acknowledge a probable death.

I glanced at Kol and Ral and Ka'a. *All will be okay*, I tried to communicate with my eyes. Though I only wanted to comfort them, I felt ashamed of my lie.

Suddenly, all sound and movement ceased. For a moment, I could hear the beating of my heart. Then a wild careening screech split the air and the still moment shattered. With a rushing shake of wings and leaves and a cacophony of mad fearful cries, our flock lurched into the clearing.

The flocks coming from the east and south had taken a head start and rushed at us as one massive black cloud. Apparently, those two flocks had banded together. Mor and Prok had fooled me—their flocks had formed an alliance. The day before, I'd somehow missed the obvious.

Jarred off-balance by this realization, I fluttered in flight and fumbled down nearly all the way to the ground. I felt I should hurry to the front of the flock and assume a position of leadership. But as I rose back up, my wing somehow got snared between two twigs on a low-hanging branch.

I gave that wing a sharp yank. Fire shot into my shoulder. Nonetheless, I didn't stop but forced myself out into the mass of squawking, screaming black bodies.

Abruptly, my muscles became short and stiff. An invisible force seemed to hold me back. Though I strained against this inertia, I soon fell to the rear of the pack. I felt so weak, so helpless.

Meanwhile, several young birds, wishing to show their courage, had sped to the front. Without hesitating, they dove into the black throng in the center of the clearing. I spotted Kol and Ral among them.

I'd expected this battle to be something like a dance—one bird squaring off against another. Respectful duels would decide the outcome.

But no—three forces collided and became a whirling chaos, a confusion stirred by the blurred flutter of black wings. Ravens smacked into one another and punched blindly with their beaks. Birds soon began plummeting down, spinning with broken limbs. Wounded bodies bounced over the ground like a rain of hail. My mind swam with vertigo, but still I forced myself forward.

At the parameter of that jumbled mass, I hung in the air, beating my wings madly, looking for a foe who was not one of our own—difficult telling who was who in that mess.

But before I could strike, something jagged and hot riveted the side of my skull. I dipped away from my unseen adversary and batted about in a stunned daze, blood blotting my vision.

For a few moments, I wobbled along at the fringe of the battle, hoping to recover enough to fight. What a shameful position for a would-be leader! Fearful that someone would attack me from the rear, I kept whirling around and jabbing the air with my beak.

Finally, a bird flew within range and I connected with a solid blow to his shoulder. I felt my beak lodge between two bones. I managed to wrench it free without falling. My victim floundered in the air, his black wing whipping out blood. He blinked at me with eyes fogged by age. In an instant, I lost all desire to fight. I saw what a fool I was!—trying to redeem myself by going full-bore into a battle I'd opposed.

A moment later, the old bird flipped backward and dropped to the ground. He rolled in agony—his wing threw sprays of blood across the sandy brown soil. I wondered if I should dive down and finish the poor bird off in an act of mercy.

Suddenly, a hard sharp beak smacked the top of my head. I tried to keep aloft—don't ask me why—but my balance rolled far to one side, then far to the other, then back again.

When I hit the ground, I tried to keep my feet by moving sideways. But before I could steady myself, all went black and a force pulled me backward and down and down and I had no strength to stop my fall.

By the time I finally awoke, the long shadows of late afternoon draped the ground. The black bodies rose into a mound five or six deep at the center of the field. Here, a wing twitched; there, a beak opened and closed in silent pain. Members of the two victorious flocks hopped about the heap, pecking at corpses and gulping down strips of flesh.

I was lost among the many—just another bloodied body lying along the fringe. I knew I must remain inconspicuous.

A bird near me struggled to his feet, then fell over sideways and began flapping his free wing helplessly.

The damp heat emanating from the dead bodies swarmed all over me. As I shifted my position, the wound on the crown of my head began to hammer with pain. My entire body felt stiff and raw in the aftermath of the terror.

To get myself free, I started pushing against the bodies around me with my talons. In this way, I managed to scoot on my belly until I reached an open patch.

Finally, I could take a fresh breath into my lungs. Using great care, I managed to get my feet under me. But in the next moment, liquid fire shot up my throat. I retched to the point of exhaustion.

After I'd recovered a bit, I crept away from the clearing, being careful not to attract attention.

I tried to locate the circle of boulders, but became disoriented and spent the night alone, hunkering in the open desert. The cold air kept my muscles tense— every fiber stung with pain. A fever rose up. I spun through a horrid sleep.

The next morning, I mustered enough strength of spirit to fly and eventually found my way back to the roost. A few of the flock hopped from boulder to boulder aimlessly. I expected to receive hateful stares and curses, but no one gave me much notice. Maybe they were no numb to care anymore.

I thought of seeking out the shaman. But no— shouldn't he come to us in such dire times?

At the family nook under the boulder I found only my sister Ka'a. She trembled in a dark corner. At first, she jumped back. Then she recognized me and relaxed a bit. I checked for physical injuries, but found only a small bald patch on her head.

Ka'a often tried to hide her vulnerability with a

flippant arrogance. In truth, she was overly romantic and tended toward dreaminess. Now all that had been stripped away.

She could not stop trembling.

"It's all right," I said softly. "It's going to be okay." I had to ease her pain somehow. I had to help her feel safe in the world again. If I couldn't, the burden of guilt I now felt might crush me.

I was desperate to ask about the others, but dared not mention them. In any case, she seemed unable to speak. Through the remainder of that day and into the night, I tried to comfort her with closeness and gentle words. Finally, the weight of physical and mental exhaustion became too much. I fell asleep.

When I awoke the next morning, Ka'a's body felt rigid beside me. The night before, she'd clung to life with all the power left to her as she shivered with shock. I felt responsible for her death—I shouldn't have let sleep get the better of me.

But I must admit, I also felt relieved. Now I could leave—leave and never return to this flock (what little remained of it). I was finally free.

"You could not have stopped that battle," I told myself. "The event had a will of its own, a will you were powerless against. Yes, we may have failed as ravens. But in the process of rebuilding itself, the flock will gain in strength—strength that will add to force of Raven.

"But my presence would only distract the others from that great task. Yes, it's best that I be gone."

With this lie, I gave myself permission to abandon the flock. No goodbyes.

* * * *

I now paused in the telling of my story...
This tale of woe had obviously touched the

sensitive neophyte deeply. Her head hung in sorrow. Maybe I needed to lighten things up a bit.

"I think now is a good time to tell the tale of Raven and Gull," I said to her. "After all, it demonstrates the value of pain.

"As the story goes..."

Our world was without light at the beginning. As a result, all the animals kept bumping into things—and each other. Often, they fell into holes.

Finally, they went to Raven and asked him to do something to solve the problem. Yes, Raven was the wisest of all creatures. And yet, the sun had been entrusted to Gull.

Unfortunately, he was a greedy bird and held the sun under his wing to keep himself warm. Though they begged him, Gull wouldn't give the other animals even a single ray of sunlight.

When Raven approached him, Gull knew what that great bird wanted. Nonetheless, he agreed to the meeting, wishing to see Raven humble himself.

"Oh wonderful Gull!" Raven sang out, standing below the rock where the bird perched. He nearly choked on his words, but forced himself to continue. "Let us—the poor creatures who cherish you—see just a bit of the sun's light. Just enough to keep us from running into one another."

"Nothing doing," said Gull. "But try me again tomorrow. And next time, don't be so stingy with the superlatives. Your pleading lacks sincerity."

Gull hopped off the rock, but as he began to walk away, he stepped on a thorn that felt like hot ragged lightning leaping into his foot.

"Blazes!" Gull shrieked. "Raven, help me. I got a thorn in my foot. Pull it out and be quick."

"Sorry," Raven said. "I can't see well enough to see

28

your foot, much less the thorn. But if you...if you...but no—I know how you feel about releasing any of the sun's light."

"Okay, okay, I'll let some go," Gull snapped. "Just pull the damn thorn." Gull lifted his wing a mere fraction. A speck of light slipped out—hardly more than the light of a star.

Raven then grabbed hold of Gull's ankle, but instead of extracting the thorn, shoved it deeper into the sensitive foot.

Gull let out a scream that shook the air. He hopped up and down on his free leg and berated Raven for his clumsiness.

"Whoops, sorry about that," Raven said. "I still can't see what I'm doing. Could you possibly—"

"Okay, okay, okay, you dolt!" Gull then raised his wing until a spot of light shone out—equal to the light of a full moon.

Nonetheless, Raven held fast to the ankle and rammed the thorn in even deeper.

"Yeeeeeeoooow!" yelled Gull. "Feathers afire. Trying to kill me, Raven?"

"Sorry, but I still don't—"

"Okay, here. Now yank that spike out before it burrows all the way up my leg!"

Gull opened his wing until the light of a sunrise fell out.

Raven then focused all his strength and with one mighty heave, sank the thorn so far into Gull's poor foot that it made the ankle bulge.

A wild commotion of expletives, threats, flapping, and feathers followed. Amid the hubbub, the sun flew out and zoomed all the way to the top of the sky, lighting up the entire Earth.

"Okay, Raven, you got your wish! Now root out the thorn!"

"You do it," Raven answered. "There's so much light, even you can see now."

Thereafter, the animals enjoyed plenty of sunlight and didn't bump into things or fall into holes. The world was a much better place for all concerned.

What's the moral of the story, you ask? Well, maybe we're like Gull: reluctant to show our light. We only open when the pain becomes too much. Then by opening, we help others to see.

Unfortunately, this story did not lighten the mood of my neophyte. She was still preoccupied with the battle between the flocks. Perhaps my loss mirrored a tragedy in her own life. Such shocks often drive a young raven into shamanism. But not me. After the battle, I merely wanted to endure life until the misery subsided.

The morning after Ka'a's death, I left the circle of boulders and flew around aimlessly. A persistent nausea kept bringing me down to the ground. In mind and heart, I'd gone numb—and took care not to stir myself up.

My first few days alone in the desert passed in this way.

But then a dream broke this false peace. I saw my family faraway in a vague white space. They stood in a loose group—together, yet separate, but uniform in the way they cocked their heads this way and that, as if confused by a strange new environment.

I called again and again, but no one responded. I walked towards them. They grew no closer. I lifted my wings to fly, but they vanished in that instant, and all when black.

After that dream, submerged feelings—feelings of guilt, of sadness, of irrevocable loss—came surging up.

In desperation, I attempted to enter The Realm of the One-In-All. Perhaps I could reconnect my family in The Realm. Maybe they'd tell me everything was okay, that I need not feel guilty.

But I felt weighted down—I could not lift out of my body. I tried for three consecutive nights.

As the days passed, I grew weaker and weaker with grief and confusion. "Maybe I should just let myself die in this empty place," I thought. I saw no other way out of my misery. No telling what other miseries might follow if I lived.

Death would return me to The Realm. But according to what I'd been told, upon arrival, I'd have to reexamine my last life on Earth and realize what I'd gotten wrong. And then see what I might do in the next life to correct those mistakes. No, Death would not give me comfort or true release.

I reminded myself that, as ravens, we accept that certain events, though painful, are a necessary part of our path. But this belief did little ease my pain—not then, not later. Though I tried to distract myself in a hundred ways, the gray cloud of that catastrophe always shadowed me. But let it be said: eventually, I worked to shrink that cloud, to shrink its shadow—if only to give myself a chance at a decent life. I stopped trying to run and instead, allowed myself to feel all the pain in its darkness and grieve over what could never be changed.

Ah, but such work is never done.

Another irony: I've spent my adult life trying to deal with the experience of a moment—what befell me, without warning, when I was still a youth.

During that dim time, I endured the stifling heat of day by searching out the darkest corner—the hang of a ledge, a nook in a boulder. Then I'd settle into lassitude and drape my thoughts in a somnolent haze.

Occasionally, dream-like images would flash in my mind: black-feathered bodies floating in thick red blood—black beaks opening wide in silent shrieks. Then I'd step from my shadow hole into the hot whiteness of day and my mind would go blind again.

After sunset, the creeping cold would slowly chill my blood and my raptor instinct would awaken. Then I'd go on the hunt. But driven by more than hunger—I found a hideous satisfaction in these kills. For some reason, I never thought about my family or the battle at night.

A foolish hope helped sustain me: the hope that some magical blessing from The Realm would touch me and I'd be cured. But I dared not hope too much. Nor did I dare ask questions about my future.

Part II

Only after many days, did the monotony of this life end. Just past sunrise on that decisive day, as I winged over the plain, I spotted three ravens perched at a cliff's edge in the distance. My heart leapt at the sight.

For a moment, I thought I'd found the surviving members of my family. The thread of deep kinship had drawn us back together again!

But no—I'd been blinded by wishful thinking. I didn't know them, those young male birds. Though they must've heard my approach, they remained frozen in place and pose as they stared across a wide canyon of sun-burnt orange and red. Odd.

I settled down on a boulder behind them and waited. Though I peered into the distance, I could not discern the object of their strong interest.

Frustrated, I finally lost patience, hopped down from my rock, and began to rustle my wings. I cleared my throat. They finally turned to look at me.

"Well, it's about time," one said. This stubby bird strode right up to me on bowed legs, looked me up and down, then trundled back to his companions. I found his cocky swagger both misplaced and amusing.

"Name is Roe," I said.

"Yeah, we're aware," the swaggering bird said.

What did he mean by that? Were they actually expecting me?

A second bird approached. He pointed his beak into the air as he said, "Allow me to introduce myself. My name is Quork. That rude upstart with whom you just spoke is Ruficollis. But we call him Rufi, though maybe he doesn't like it much. That other fellow, the ragged one there, is Squee." Quork had a long slender neck—quite unusual on a raven. I smiled at his affected sophistication.

Squee kept his distance, but beaded his stare at me, while nodding his head and shuffling his wings. Incredibly scruffy for a raven, he was. His neck feathers were splayed out and his tail feathers crisscrossed at awkward angles. A weird, convoluted energy emanated from him.

"You guys belong to a flock out here or what?" I asked.

"No, we're alone," Quork said. "Shamans-in-training, that's what we are." He puffed out his scrawny chest with pride.

"Okay, but what'd you do exactly?"

"We're learning the dance of life."

"You mean you play?"

Rufi cut me a hard narrow look. "It's rough out here," he cawed. "The training. The trials. The hazards. You need the will and strength of a mountain goat; the patience and flexibility of a snake; the alertness and quickness of a jackrabbit."

"We're treading on the edge of the world out here," Quork said. "The things we're discovering—it's truly amazing."

"Okay, whatever." Though I felt desperate for company, I didn't wish to get drawn into their games.

"Well, I guess I'll go now and let you get back to what you were doing."

"If you're here, you're here for a reason," Quork said quickly. "Obviously, you're supposed to stay and learn as we do."

"I assure you I'm not cut out for the job. Anyway, I have no desire for such pursuits right now. I lost my flock and family in a tragic event recently."

To my chagrin, they didn't seem the least bit interested in my story of woe. I wanted to unburden myself—confess my guilt.

"At least talk to our shaman before you go," Quork said.

"Oh, you have a shaman here?"

"Well, of course! Shamans-in-training must be taught by an experienced shaman."

Without another question, I agreed to this meeting. In my current state of passivity and bleariness and confusion and disillusionment, I desired guidance —guidance more than meaning.

I just hoped their shaman wouldn't tell me to join these three. Yes, a shaman is the most respected bird of the flock; the main source of information, both trivial and profound. But during her youth, she's usually what you'd call a "doofus". An ill-fitting tooth in the jaw of life. Such ill-fitting teeth eventually accept their oddness and become shamans. I didn't want to think of myself in those terms. I wanted to be special, yes, but not strange.

The three would-be shamans took me to their roost —a place of jumbled rock and sagebrush at the base of a cliff. A small spring snaked through the shrubbery.

They kept back as I approached a low cavern in the cliff. After several moments of polite waiting, I heard a tired shuffling and the dry, scraping sound of tail feathers in cave dust. The old shaman stopped near the entrance, keeping to the shadows. His dark eyes had an outer layer of transparent gray.

"So why'd you bring him here?" he asked his trio.

"We thought you wanted us to," Quork said, having suddenly lost his haughtiness.

"Oh yeah, I guess I did," said the shaman. "Well, I have nothing more to say to him."

Without another word, the cantankerous relic turned and waddled back into the darkness of the cave.

The three shamans-in-training looked both confused and embarrassed. Their esteemed leader had just shown himself to be a dull rusty pigeon of a bird.

Though my questions remained unanswered, I did feel relieved regarding one thing: if I was meant to be a shaman, their master would've told me.

Comforted by that thought, I begin to nettle the neophytes. "Well?" I asked them. "What's with that addled ancient of yours?"

"He has mysterious ways," Rufi said defensively.

"Yeah, well, *my* way leads me out of there," I told them.

"You can't just go," Squee said.

"Why not?"

"Because the shaman predicted you'd come here," Quork announced dramatically, flourishing his wings.

"He told us about you," Rufi added. "He actually gave your name. Whatever you may think, he's a great shaman."

"Not anymore," I said. "He should retire."

Rufi rushed at me then, but I stepped up to meet him. We stood beak to beak, eyeball to eyeball. If he wanted a fight, I was ready. I craved an outlet for my frustration.

After holding my stare for a long tense moment, Rufi looked away, toward a passing cloud, then turned on his toes and strolled off, feigning nonchalance. He was tough, but smart as well—he could see I was wild in the head.

Then Squee took wing and shot back to the top of the cliff. His companions followed. I considered diving into the cave and demanding some answers from that ramshackle puff-chest. But I couldn't unlearn the respect I'd been taught.

Though disappointed, I decided to stay at this place awhile longer. To be honest, I was a little lonely. And I didn't have any other plans except to keep flying. "No reason to rush," I told myself. "Besides, though I'm not going to become one of them, I'm interested in how these novices train."

Nonetheless, I didn't want to act too friendly. Didn't want to get their hopes up. So I waited a few moments more, then flew back to the top of the cliff. I settled down a short way behind the amateur shamans.

They didn't stir, but stared out over the sun-blasted canyon, just as before. Waves of heat liquefied the air. My tongue now felt dry and stiff. What the hell were they looking at or for?

Finally, I said, "Yes, that's a nice canyon—those ragged rock formations, those walls of stone with their ripples of burnt-orange and bleached brown. But why gaze at it all day long?"

The three rookies said nothing, but continued to peer across the canyon toward the white horizon. They appeared quite solemn, quite studious, as befitted their status as shamans-in-training. My frustration started to rise again. Then Squee said, "Part of our training."

"Well yeah, but what's the purpose?"

"We are developing our seeing," he replied.

That was surely the dumbest thing I'd ever heard. All ravens are born with superbly keen, intelligent eyesight—an optical power beyond any other creature.

"Okay, whatever."

Rufi ruffled at my sarcasm. "We aren't looking for something. We're trying to *see*. A big difference there."

"What're you trying to see that you can't see already?"

"This physical world of ours is but one world," Quork said.

"Sure, everybody knows that."

"No, I'm not referring to The Realm. I'm talking about a land beyond our own."

"A Land?" I asked.

"Yes, a land," Squee said eagerly. "Just four days ago I visited part of that land—the part known as The Land of the Dead. I did, I really did. I saw an opening—hard to describe, it's like a movement in space—and I went for it. Then suddenly there I was: the Land of the Dead."

"The Land of the Dead?"

"Yeah, where we all go, at least for awhile, right after we die."

"That's where we review the life that's just past?"

"I don't know. I don't know what the dead do there. The shaman hasn't said. He just said there's where I went."

An idea suddenly came to me. "My family would be in that land right now," I said. "I really need to settle things with them. Make sure everything's alright. They died so suddenly. Okay, so where's that opening, Squee? Guide me to it. Guide me through it. Just show me what I have to do. You said you wanted me to join in your training, right? Well okay then."

"You're a newbie, pal," Rufi said. "You got to start out slow and work your way up."

"You must go through a process of development first," Quork added.

"I'm not asking either of you. Squee's the one that went there. If indeed he actually did."

"Hey, I'm proud of what I accomplished. A shaman-in-training like me entering The Land of the Dead? That's something special. In fact, I could've gone yesterday, if I'd wanted. I saw the opening again. I didn't go, because you see, once you're in, you've got to find your way back out. A little tricky, yeah. I was lucky. Others haven't been so lucky. So I've been told."

"Don't worry about me," I assured him. "I just want to see my family again. I need to see them again. I don't really care what happens to me after that. You said I came here for a reason. Well, this must be the reason."

Receiving no response, I continued, "Listen Squee, in order to become a shaman, you must learn to be decisive. You must learn to rely on your own deep spirit for guidance. You can't rely on anything, anyone else—

not Rufi or Quork or even your old shaman. Listen to your spirit."

I knew I had him; somehow I knew the other two couldn't hold him back.

Even so, I felt I shouldn't press too hard. An awkward pause followed. The three junior shamans searched the ground at their feet for a few moments, then turned back to the cliff's edge. Again, they stared across the canyon toward the white horizon. With nothing else to do for the moment, I joined them.

The heat of midday broasted our shiny black feathers. I knew a slow hot afternoon lay before us. Yet I now felt an uplift of spirit. I had a purpose beyond mere survival.

Though I pretended to try to see, I kept sneaking sidelong glances at Squee. Waiting.

Quork suddenly broke the silence. "Squee, you should at least ask the shaman first."

"He knows what you're about to do," I told Squee. "He understands why I'm here. He just wants you to use your own initiative, that's all. It's a test."

A few moments later, Squee dove off the cliff and took wing in a northerly direction. I dropped from our perch and followed.

As Squee and I sailed across the canyon, he kept on squinting his eyes and peering into the distance. I tried to learn more about the process of entering lands, but he ignored me.

I soon discovered how much my confused sojourn in the desert had weakened me. My wings began to feel so heavy. My rib cage ached as I struggled for breath. I became lost in the strain of my exertions.

After I don't know how long, I turned my attention back out again and found we'd entered a shadowy land. In this twilight world, roiling gray clouds completely obscured the sky above. Distant plateaus and buttes appeared as silhouettes against a black background.

Squee suddenly dropped down into a forest, sooty gray in the dusk. I followed. We came to rest on the bank of a river black as a black snake. Fog drifted through a stand of trees across the water.

"Okay," I whispered, "what now?"

"We can not enter by ourselves. They must come for us." He eyed those trees with fierce intensity—no longer the doofus I'd first met; more of a warrior now. "Remember," he said, "everything that happens here happens as it's meant to happen. If you make a mistake, it's a mistake you were supposed to make."

I felt even more confused, but decided to let all questions rest for the time being.

Abruptly, Squee cawed three times. The sound echoed down the dark sliding waters. Again, he lifted his beak and cawed three times, then again three times, then again. We waited. The fog began to creep across the water toward us. Still no response from the other side.

The smoky gray twilight shifted to the darkness of night. A full moon rose above the trees and put a white streak over the black river.

Faraway cries and caws and screechings now sounded through the trees. Ravens all talking at once.

Squee raised his beak and began to sing. The raven commotion silenced at once. Without thinking, I lifted my beak and began to sing along with him. Though I'd always enjoyed singing, my vocal abilities were limited.

But now the notes just flowed from my throat—dense as honey, yet free as a rising breeze.

Squee's song and my song became one song, a song issuing from us, yet not of our creation—a song using us. Its layered sounds conveyed the feeling of a journey of longing, a journey of a pain, the pain that comes from desire. We sang of the secret feelings of all, feelings never spoken because such feelings go beyond words. We sang of the hidden wound, a wound so obvious.

Then, after I don't know how long, our song ended.

As I came back to myself, my attention shifted to the river. I spied a canoe immersed in fog moving toward us on the water. Four ravens, working in sync, stirred the fog with their paddles.

After the canoe struck our bank, we stepped aboard with cautious feet. The four ravens then began to row back to the opposite side, where a crowd waited for us. My heart sank a bit when I did not see my family among them. But I refused to lose hope.

After we landed, an old woman raven with swollen knees and a blunt beak approached me. "Why have you come here?" she asked tenderly. "You are not supposed to be here among us."

"I'm here for my family," I said. "They were taken from me. They died too soon, I'm sure."

"They will return in time," she said. "They will return when it's time for them to return. Just as the leaves return when it's time for them to return in spring."

"But their death was my fault. I should be here, not them. Perhaps we can arrange an exchange."

"No—all is as it should be. They will return in time."

"Well, at least let me stay here awhile and be in their company."

"Okay, but you can not speak to them nor can you touch them," the old woman raven said. "Stay here by the river and we will send for you. We have much to do this evening."

The ravens then turned together and disappeared into the deeper darkness of the trees. Though I'd acquiesced to the old woman, I'd not given up on my plan.

As Squee and I waited, the full moon rose to its zenith. That white circle then began to expand. Soon, the moon nearly filled the night sky, bathing us in a mist of soft light.

We could now hear a deep rumble of drums in the distance—hurried beats, densely-layered, booming through the trees—growing in intensity, with wave after wave sounding through our bodies, striking us to the core. I could not think.

After I don't know how long, the drumming shut down abruptly. An extended moment of silence followed. Then I began to hear the sound of many raven feet marching, scraping over bare earth. Scraw-scraw-scraw-STOMP. Scraw-scraw-scraw-STOMP. Scraw-scraw-scraw-STOMP.

Three young ravens came to Squee and I and led us along a path through the trees. We ended at a clearing where a hundred or more dead ravens had gathered to dance. The males danced in the outer circle. The females danced in the inner circle. The males all moved in one direction. The females all moved in the opposite. Their shadows cut across the ground in wild, flaring shapes. Scraw-scraw-scraw-STOMP. Scraw-scraw-scraw-STOMP. Scraw-scraw-scraw-STOMP.

My eyes raced through the marching group, but found no one from my family. Perhaps they were still among living.

The three ravens set a big pot of seal oil before my companion and me. When the tangy, wet smell hit our nostrils, hunger seized us and we sank our beaks into the oil. That liquid was light flowing into my body; that light absorbed my lingering sense of illness. For the moment, I felt content.

Suddenly, the marchers halted their steps and knelt down with heads bowed. A young raven stood at their center. This small bird began to sing. Her delicate notes had the whimsy of dandelion balls dancing on a breeze. They seemed so slight, yet I felt wounded by their perfection.

To my surprise, I realized the singer was Ka'a, my sister.

Five ravens came up and formed a circle around her: Grandfather, Father, Mother, and my brothers, Kal and Rol.

On impulse, I tried to answer Ka'a's song, but my voice rasped a harsh moan. With my notes, the moment and everything in it suddenly froze—all the ravens and even the leaves on the trees—even the moonlight filtering down through the air.

With a stiff cracking sound, that light splintered and fell, littering the clearing with ice-like shards. My foul sound had wrecked the ritual. I felt such shame!

"Quick," Squee said. "We must use this moment to gather your family together so we can return them to the Land of the Living. Let's put them in this oil pot."

"They'll fit?"

"With room to spare."

"Then perhaps we could bring everyone back," I said, without thinking. "Otherwise, it wouldn't be fair."

And so, we began loading the bodies of all the dead ravens into the oil pot, grabbing each by the nape of the neck with our beaks. Oddly enough, those bodies were as thin as leaves and as light.

After its beams had broken apart, the full moon had shrunk back down to normal size. So I now fumbled in the dark, all the while worried that the moment might suddenly unfreeze.

At the end of our labors, I added Grandfather, then Father and Mother, then Kol and Ral, and finally Ka'a to the top layer of ravens in the pot. The flock, in its entirety, only covered the bottom of the vessel.

Squee and I slid the lid back on, made it snug, then hauled the pot to the canoe.

We moved away from the bank, dipping our paddle blades into the hovering fog without touching the water. In the distance, a gray streak along the horizon signaled the approach of dawn.

"Hurry," Squee said. "We must reach the far bank before sunrise or else the dead must return to the The Land of the Dead."

But no matter how we worked the paddles, no matter how hard we strained, the canoe cruised along at the same moderate speed. A glow of deep red now appeared on the horizon—steadily spreading; throwing pink-yellow rays up into the sky.

A low rumbling came from inside the seal oil pot.

"What's happening?" I asked.

"With the rising of the sun, the raven bodies expand. Soon, they'll be at full size."

The pot began to jitter with vibration on the bottom of the boat. The jitter became a rattle, then the rattle became a blurry shake.

A slice of gold sun peeked above the horizon. I could hear muffled voices within the oil pot shout, "Let us out! Open the jar, you crows! It's getting cramped in here."

"Spirits be silent!" Squee cawed. "You'll be free in a moment. Relax!"

The pot quieted. The bank was now just a short swoop away. Squee and I sighed with relief and dipped our paddles down one more time.

But then the sun—a sudden bubble—appeared full-blown over the horizon. In the same moment, the pot lid popped off and high-pitched keening stung our ears. Raven bodies shot up into the air and for a suspended breath, became a tall black bouquet. Then in the next instant, they all rained down into the water like a fall of volcanic rock. A river wave slapped our canoe on one side and another wave slapped it on the other. Then a third wave heaved the boat way up, flipped it over, then threw it back down, shoving Squee and I underwater.

I flopped about for some time before I finally managed to reach the shore. My wet feathers dripped gold in the morning sun. I found Grandfather and Father and Mother and Kol and Ral and Ka'a bobbing in the river, along with all the other dead ravens. "Come on," I shouted, "you can make it. You can return to The Land of the Living."

"No, son," Father said. "Leaves can not return in winter. They must wait until spring. We can not go with you. We've are now in a new cycle of life."

"But you left me much too soon," I said.

"All is as it needs to be."

I watched silently as the current pulled them back to the other side, back to The Land of the Dead. One by one, my family climbed onto the bank and shook the water from their wings in a blur of silver spray.

For several moments, we gazed at one another across the river as the fog began to thicken again. Strangely, I felt a stronger connection now than when they still lived. For the first time, I realized that in any union there is love—even when the union appears to produce its opposite.

One by one, the members of my family turned from me and entered the darkness of the trees.

"Well," Squee said, "I guess that settles that."

Then, without waiting a moment longer, the shaman-in-training raised his wings and ascended into the sky.

I wanted to sit with my grief awhile, but knew I needed to follow him. I felt as if I was fighting against the pull of an invisible thread as I flew. For all my furious flapping, I made little forward progress. But finally, after a much effort, I came within shouting distance of Squee.

"Hey, slow down," I yelled. "Can't you wait? I need a break."

Though he must've heard me, he kept flying at the same pace. Soon, Squee was nothing more than a black dot against the backdrop of a dark blue sky becoming light blue.

The sun now blazed with the new energy of morning.

With the loss of Squee, my spirit dropped to nothing. After a short time, I gave up and settled down to the desert floor. The ground was quickly heating up. So barren here. Not a boulder or even some sagebrush to provide a shadow. By mid-morning, my body smoldered like a coal.

"If this is my undoing—my end—then so be it," I said to myself. "I'm ready to leave the earth realm. Yeah, I know I'll have to examine this life and realize my mistakes. But I'd rather look at it from a distance, than live it up close."

I fell on my back and concentrated on sucking enough air out of the heat to keeping on breathing. I closed my eyes and saw the sun in red circles behind my lids.

I knew death would come slowly and resigned myself to the painful tedium.

But soon after I settled in, I became aware of a faint humming sound. This high-pitched hum then began to intensify, coming steadily closer, until its metallic whine bore right into my head. I popped an eye open, hoping to shut off the source, if possible.

A hummingbird hovered over me, dipping and darting in that erratic way they have. I wanted to ask the tiny bird what it was doing in the middle of a harsh desert, but it spoke first.

"Why do you rest here?" the hummingbird asked with its small high voice. "I would think it somewhat unpleasant under this sun."

"Hummingbird," I said, "I am tired, thirsty, sore, and sad. I've resigned myself to dying in this place. Please, leave me alone with my pain."

"Don't be so impulsive," it said. "Listen to me and you'll be okay. Go north a short distance and you'll find a valley and in that valley, a gorge, and in that gorge, a stream. After you take a drink of its sweet water, follow the stream—again going due north. The stream will fork and when it does, follow the branch to the west. Do not, I repeat, do not, go down the east branch."

As a raven, I was not accustomed to taking instruction from hummingbirds. A decorative creature, yes; useful to some degree, true. But, to my mind, more insect than bird in habit and demeanor.

"Promise me you won't take the branch to the east," the hummingbird said.

"Okay, yeah, sure, I promise."

"Good. And one other thing: do not, I repeat, do not take a blanket from any of the boulders you find on the branch to the west."

"Rocks with blankets?"

"Yes."

"Why would I want a blanket in this heat?"

"Just do as I say or you'll be sorry."

"Okay, but where will that branch lead me?"

"It'll lead you where you need to go."

In the next moment, the hummingbird shot up and away and was soon less than a speck in that bleached-blue sky.

I then gathered together what remained of my strength and took flight.

A valley a short distance away, the hummingbird had said. I saw no valley—nothing but flat naked desert all the way to the horizon.

But then, when I next looked down, I found a wide valley below me and a gorge in that valley and a stream snaking its way through that gorge.

I didn't wait but swooped down and took a long drink from the stream. The cool water not only refreshed my body but also my being. I paused and breathed in a breeze scented by the small pine trees along the bank. Feeling nearly like myself again, I took a stroll through the gorge, heading due north.

Soon, I came to the branch in the stream. At first, my curiosity pulled me toward the branch to the east. But then I remembered the boulders with blankets on the branch going west.

So I ambled down that branch until I came to knoll that rose from the bank. Atop that small hill stood a scatter of boulders, all roughly rectangular in shape. A brightly-colored blanket covered each one—as if they were all asleep.

A red blanket with thick black stripes lay draped over one boulder. Another boulder wore a dark blue blanket with orange and white stripes. A third was hidden by a magenta blanket with thin yellow stripes. No two boulders had blankets of the same color and design. But in one way their blankets were all the same: each was made of the same high-grade wool, woven to create a rich texture.

Of course, I knew I didn't need a blanket. But I also knew I'd take one. I just have to have one. Was it fair to ask me to reject such beauty?

So I grabbed the blanket nearest me—crimson in color, black and white striped—and hurried back down the knoll to the gorge.

Naturally, I couldn't fly with that heavy blanket on my back. But nothing bad had happened when I took the blanket. So maybe I was safe. That hummingbird was probably trying to fool me, hoping to keep all those blankets for itself.

But after I'd walked a short spell, I detected an odd noise coming from behind me. Sounded like small pebbles being ground together. The earth beneath my feet began to tremble. Turning, I spotted a long narrow boulder rolling lengthwise through the gorge toward me. Intuitively, I knew if I dropped the blanket, the boulder would stop and leave me be. But I couldn't bring myself to surrender the blanket so easily. Such fine tight texture! And those deeply-saturated colors! It was luscious, it was.

I started up a hill. When I reached the top, I looked back to check on the boulder. That stubborn rock had pushed itself halfway up the incline. I wagged the blanket at it, just as a tease, then scampered down the other side.

At the bottom, I checked again. The boulder hadn't made the crest yet. I started to feel safe once more. In any case, I knew I could easily out-run that stone. So I held the blanket close and followed another stream through another gorge.

But when I next stopped for water, I again heard that grinding sound, that rumble. Faint, but unmistakable. I dreaded to look but I looked anyway. Yes—there in the far distance, the boulder trundled down the gorge, moving slowly but steadily toward me. That stupid rockhead!

I continued along the stream for awhile, then took a big breath and began a steep climb up the side of a plateau. Halfway to the top, I stopped to look and found the boulder still clumping through the gorge. But if that stone would not relent, neither would I—I, after all, was Raven!

Besides, that blanket had come to me as if borne by destiny. Draped over my shoulder, it felt so perfect, so natural, as if made especially for me.

At the top of the plateau, I checked the boulder's progress again. It struggled at the base, rotating as if moving in place. Surely, the incline would be much too steep for the stone. It might stall there forever, refusing to concede.

Easing my pace, I walked to the other end of the plateau, then wove my way down to another gorge. As I dragged my tired feet through the pebbles and dust, I felt safe enough to daydream. I almost forgot time...until, once again, I heard the grinding sound behind me. Painfully familiar! Apparently, that damn boulder could go on forever. And I couldn't. I felt near the end of my strength even now. Muscles cried from a deep stinging sensation. My heart shuddered and coughed with its efforts. Sand had slowly filled my lungs.

"Sooner or later, I'll stumble and knock myself out and then the rock will have me," I thought.

I managed to push myself up out of the gorge and up the side of a hill. Halfway to the top, I just had to sit down and catch my breath.

After my bleary eyes had cleared a bit, I caught sight of a mountain sheep standing nearby. Its muscled chest spoke of physical prowess.

"Hello, Raven," the sheep said, with its dark round eyes full of happy innocence. "Tell me, what's that slung across your back?"

"That, my brother, is a blanket."

"You're very lucky to own something so wonderful."

"Yes, I am, but alas, all is not well. A boulder has chased me 'til I'm badly worn. It wants to steal my blanket. Tell me, is that right? Is that decent? Can you help me?"

"Why, of course I can. Of course, I will. After all, I am monarch of this mountain. How dare that boulder torment my friends! Where is it?"

"Just wait. It'll be here soon."

I moved off to the side and bided my time. The sheep raked its curlicue horns against a dead tree trunk and scraped the ground with its hooves. As the boulder began grinding its way up the steep slope, the sheep shouted, "Halt! This is my mountain. Defend yourself."

But the boulder kept rolling, moving faster now—as if spurred by a raging anger.

The sheep danced back a few steps, pointed its head, then shot straight at the rock.

But when that iron-hard head hit the stone, the sheep's strong body went limp, flipped into the air, then slapped down on the ground like a wad of mud. And the boulder kept on churning up the hill.

"Thanks for trying," I yelled to the mountain sheep. "Sorry, but I must be going."

Once again, I heaved my way up the hillside as the boulder crunched through the gravel and scree, staying close behind me. "If you go back home, I'll return the blanket tomorrow," I shouted over my shoulder. "I only need it this evening, to keep me warm just this one night."

But the rock wouldn't be fooled. No—if anything, it bore down even harder.

I knew I should just drop the blanket. But life seemed so much better with it than without it. And I really needed a better life right now. Besides, how could such a boorish stone appreciate this fine blanket?

When I reached the top of the hill, I did not pause, but began to scoot down the other side. At the bottom, a cottonmouth snake sunned itself on a flat slab beside a bubbling spring.

"Dear snake," I said, gasping for breath, "I need your assistance. I'm being chased by a boulder that wants nothing less than to kill me. Please, can you help?"

"I can and I will, my brother." The snake narrowed its yellow eyes at the boulder barreling down the mountain. "I will clasp that rock between my powerful jaws and crush it to death."

The cottonmouth lifted its head with mouth open wide. A moment later, the boulder landed at the spring with an earth-shaking thud. The snake then leapt forward in a flash and clamped those trap-like jaws on a small knob protruding from the stone.

As the snake held fast, the boulder kept on rolling. The monolith flipped the snake around a few times, then mashed it asunder several more. Finally, the cottonmouth gave up and let go.

Lying motionless on the ground, that pulpy-red reptile gave me a dull stare. Its tongue hung limply from the side of its mouth.

"Thanks for trying," I yelled to the snake. "Sorry, but I must be going."

I now raced across the desert with the boulder in close pursuit. A hare stood on its hind legs, watching us.

"Don't worry," it shouted. "I will stop that stone with my paws."

The big-eared creature braced itself. In the next moment, it ricocheted off the rock and went airborne in a wide arc. As a puff bag of fur, it bounced and bounced across the ground before finally rolling to a stop.

"Thanks for trying," I yelled to the hare.

Next, I spotted a deer grazing on desert grass. It offered to catch the stone with its antlers. Though I knew quite well what would happen, for some reason, I did not object.

Of course, those antlers snapped like dry twigs as the boulder plowed forward.

I felt outdone and done-out. Nonetheless, I strained my poor legs and managed to put some space between myself and my adversity. Then, as I paused for a quick breath, I detected that hum again. That irritating high-pitched whine.

I looked up to see the hummingbird hovering overhead. "Well well well," the little bird said.

In the distance, a dust cloud spiraled into the air as the boulder continued to toil toward me.

"I'm in no mood for lectures," I told the hummingbird. "Just help me out of this fix. That is, if you can."

"Why don't you just give up the blanket?"

"I wish I could, but I can't. I know it's just a blanket. I know it's caused me problems. Even so, I can't seem to let go of it."

"Well, I really shouldn't help you, but here goes."

The hummingbird made a straight line for the boulder. When it stopped above the rock, the rock also stopped. A sharp thin hum then issued from the tiny bird. The stone begin to tremble. Its trembling intensified into a sustained shudder. My ears stung with the steady piercing sound. Soon I heard a harsh moan—so full of pain it touched my heart. The boulder grew still. In the next moment, it cracked neatly down the middle. What was once one was now two separate pieces. A transparent-green amoebic form wavered and wiggled above the halves for a moment, then drifted upward and soon disappeared into the gathering dusk.

"What was that?" I called to the hummingbird.

"The spirit of the boulder."

"The spirit of the boulder?"

"Yes. The boulder had a spirit. Not a spirit like you or I have, but a spirit nonetheless."

"And now?"

"Now what you see before you are two pieces of plain rock. You don't have to worry: neither will chase you." Without another word, the hummingbird shot up and away, lost into the sky.

I stared at the broken boulder a few moments more, then began to walk. Having grown weary of using my feet, I soon hung the blanket on the arm of a cactus and took flight.

Oddly enough, I didn't feel much remorse over what I'd just done. Nor did I worry about what to do next or in what direction I should travel. I flew merely for the sake of flying.

That evening I plopped my sore limbs down on the flat top of a butte and fell right into a deep well of sleep.

The next morning, I woke refreshed and watched with pleasure as the desert turned dusky red with the coming of first light.

For a goodly while, I didn't feel like doing anything and so, I did nothing at all. I gave little consideration to where I'd been or what I'd done. I was at peace with my thoughts, because I really didn't have much going on in my head.

Of course, such peace does not last for those who are not truly at peace. My sweet daze dissipated when a "V" of geese made a sharp dive and came down to land at the other end of the butte.

First, the father flapped to stop, then the mother, then their five offspring—one of whom was the prettiest non-raven female I'd ever seen.

To be honest, we ravens have often ridiculed the geese. As we see it, they lack sophistication—but perhaps the better word is "depth".

Generally, ravens see the goose as a barely cognizant being: it eats, it excretes, it mindlessly copulates. North for the summer. South for the winter. Every year, the same old routine. Not that we have anything against migratory birds—if that's your thing, so be it, we say. But in regards to the goose, migration seemed to be just another dumb habit in its status quo existence.

Yes, I accepted these ideas at the time. And yet I couldn't keep my eyes off that lovely young female. I watched with fascination as she stretched out that long slender neck, displaying her brilliant orange beak to perfection. Her manner, her moves, lacked any trace of affectation. "The source of such elegance must be the beauty of her spirit," I told myself.

I knew the family would soon take flight, so I skipped right on over and introduced myself to the father.

"Sir," I said, "your fair daughter—the one with the elegant neck—is the rainbow that follows the rain. Her eyes unite day with night. Her deep heart echoes the answer to the question in my own deep heart. Father, I wish to marry her— if she will have me, and I assure you, I will do all I can to convince her of my sincerity and worth."

The old gander crooked his neck and peered down his silly bill at me. Then he waddled two steps one way, then he waddled two steps back. Then again, he peered down his silly bill.

"You sure don't resemble any goose I've ever seen," he finally said.

"No kidding," I thought to myself, but told him, "Sir, to be honest, I am a raven, not a goose. But as I see it, your daughter and I are both birds, so what's the big deal?"

"Geese are geese and ravens are ravens. And my daughter must marry a goose."

Of course, I knew he was right. But my heart demanded that I persist. "Father, if I leave here now, the love I feel will pain me to the end of my days. Are you going to damn me to such torture? Here's my proposition: allow me to accompany you and your family for the next few days. In that time, I know you'll come to see the strength of my intent, and the nobleness of my heart. Wise bird that you are, I'm sure you'll then accept my union with your daughter as a blessing, despite our superficial differences."

He blinked at me with those small dumb eyes and blinked again, struggling to comprehend. Finally he said, "Okay, sooty tyro, I tell you what: migrate south with us. Show me you can make the trip. If you endure the crossing, then we'll talk some more about your idea of marriage."

My spirit lifted to the heavens. "I'm in," I thought to myself.

The old one introduced me to his family and told them of my plan. As a westerly wind began to stir, we didn't waste time, but lifted our wings and took flight.

The seven geese flew in a rigid "V" with the father in the lead. The long-neck daughter brought up the rear on one side. I moved up beside her.

I began my work with a stream of idle chitchat— casual observations just to get a flow going between us. But apparently, she was a bird of few words. Bashful, it seemed. How could I get her to open to me? Maybe I could provoke a little sympathy.

I then began to tell her about my restless fledglinghood. Then about the drought that had led to the destruction of my family and flock. I sang a sorrowful tune, I did.

"And so, I have wandered alone ever since," I told her. "Lost. Struggling to heal. Struggling to make sense of this life. Until now, that is. My path, I realize now, is blessed because, though painful, it has led me to this blessing. The blessing that is you."

Oh, that made her gulp hard! After composing herself, my bride-to-be managed to speak. "The story of your suffering has touched my heart in way unfamiliar to me. Perhaps this is what they mean when they say 'love'. As a raven, you naturally have many disgusting habits. And yet, I feel you have much good in you; I feel you are capable of change. Thus, I will accept you as my husband."

"Dearest dear wife, my life is now a golden morning sun. And yet, I still see one cloud: your father doesn't seem so keen on this union. You think he'll keep the agreement we made?"

"I'll handle father."

A sweet-scented breeze now lifted my wings. My body surged with new energy. Suddenly, I realized how tired I'd been, how heavy I'd felt. In a single moment, all my cares—the great burden I held within—had fallen away. Never to return—or so I believed.

"You won't be disappointed," I told her. "I swear, I promise. We'll get married as soon as possible, and then...and then..." How could I tell her that she must leave her family? After consummating the marriage, we would look for an accommodating raven flock, a mature group that would accept a sophisticated arrangement.

"But before we can become husband and wife, we must first reach the south," she said. "And to do that, we must cross the perilous Clapping Mountains."

"No problem," I said. "The strength of our love will carry us through." I didn't want to consider any potential hazard at the moment. I only wanted to maintain this bliss.

Unfortunately, I was unused to flying all day without a break. I must admit, that great upsurge of love faded a little as fatigue began to creep into my limbs. I fell back a couple of wingspans. But then I flapped a bit harder and caught up again. However, the wind now seemed to be working against me. I slid back three wingspans, then four. Though I strained with all my might, I slipped farther and farther behind. Oddly enough, but my fiancé didn't once glance back to check on me. I realized I might lose track of the goose family completely.

"What's wrong, son?" the father called to me, his voice made small by the distance.

"Nothing...not...a...thing," I wheezed. "Don't worry... about me...I'll make it...I hurt...my wing yesterday...that's all." A lie, but I was desperate.

"Sorry to hear that," the father said. "But we can not slow down. We're on a deadline, you see. No time to waste."

"Not...a problem," I panted. "Go on...ahead...I'll catch up."

But as the sun dipped behind the mountains, the silhouetted "V" of those geese merged with the darkening twilight sky. I couldn't even hear their obnoxious honking.   I'd lost my bride, and with her, my hope and the fire of my spirit. For awhile, I just glided along aimlessly.

Then I happened to look down to see a smooth lake covered with a red sheen by the setting sun. And on that lake, I saw a family of seven geese swimming in a single file line.

"Oh hello, son," the father said, as I swooped down over them. He sounded none too pleased. "We'll rest here on the lake for the evening."

"You said 'on the lake'?"

"Yes, *on* the lake."

"Sorry, but I can't stay afloat all night the way you do. Perhaps someone has a back I can sleep on?"

"Well, yes, of course. Get a good rest, because tomorrow we must cross the perilous Clapping Mountains."

I began to drift toward my beloved as nonchalantly as possible. But then the old patriarch crooked his neck, peered down his silly bill at me, and said, "No son, you will sleep on my back tonight."

I must admit I felt quite cozy among all those thick, warm feathers. But unfortunately, we woke much too early and took flight almost immediately. My wings and back were as stiff as oak wood from the previous day's exertions. The goose family was soon way ahead of me. But I wasn't about to give up.

"Once I work out the soreness, I'll be alright," I thought. "Then I just have to get over those Clapping Mountains. I wonder what makes them so perilous anyway? How could they be any more dangerous than other mountains? I've been in mountains before. I'm not scared of any mountains."

Around mid-morning, the silhouette of the Clapping Mountains finally broke the line of the horizon. Peaks of a uniform height serrated the sky. From a distance, they looked like any other mountain range. But as I drew closer, I noticed some peculiar activity. Those mountaintops seemed to move like field of restless waves.

Focusing my keen vision, I soon detected the reason for that illusion: each sharp skinny peak would split in half, then in the next moment, slap back together again. Then split again, then slap back together again. A skyline of beaks opening and closing, opening and closing. Yes: they did clap. But not in sync.

Black clouds hovered directly above the range. A frosty wind shot through my feathers and chilled my skin.

Nonetheless, I did not falter in my resolve, but pushed ahead with greater urgency. As long as I maintained an even flight, how could those peaks hurt me?

I couldn't see the family now; I'd worry about them later. I was sure I could find those fools again.

As I crossed the border separating plain from range, I tried to increase my altitude. But the clouds seemed press me back down. Below, the jaws of the Clapping Mountains swung open, then slammed shut, swung open, then slammed shut—each one giving a glimpse of a pitch-black abyss within.

A strong wind began to blow, knocking me to and fro with its ferocity. I flapped my wings furiously, but to no avail against that merciless gale. I began to drop.

Sorrowful moans echoed from those mountain as they opened. What a cacophony!—a field of hurt!

At this rushing rate of descent, I knew I'd soon fall victim to a hungry peak. In a last desperate effort, I summoned all my strength and pushed my wings down as I pointed my body straight up.

Though I did gain the safety of some altitude, when the next peak opened below me, it created a vacuum and I was sucked back down again.

Once again, I fought and managed to climb up. But again—and too soon—the vacuum of another mountain mouth drew me down.

I went through this routine again and again and again. Needing all my energy just to stay aloft, I made little forward progress and each time I slipped, I came that much closer to a snapping beak.

At this point, I no longer cared a whit about my spindly-neck bride. Where was she when I needed her? With her family, of course. I could see where her priorities lie.

A spiraling wind caught me suddenly and slung me around and down. I flapped my wings frantically, but the funnel grew even fiercer. I kept on spinning downward, straight toward an open mountain peak. Its moan and my moan chorused together in a forlorn howl.

Then, with a sharp clap the peak shut and I shot straight up on a blast of air.

But when I hit the ceiling of cloud, another whirlwind drew me down, toward the mouth of another Clapping Mountain.

Once again, the peak slapped shut before I was crushed, creating a gust that pushed me back up.

And so it went: thrown around by those winds, I escaped death time and again—always by the narrowest of margins.

I knew I'd never get across the mountains at this rate. My wings were useless in such turbulence.

Finally, I decided to surrender. Why prolong my suffering? I would aim myself straight down into the next mountain that opened below me. Easy enough. This way, I'd go of my own accord.

I then folded my wings in, pointed my beak down, and shut my eyes, feeling quite at peace with my decision. Then I stopped...I should make a final statement before I left this life. A few words to add dignity to an existence that seemed to lack any. Well, as I saw it, though I'd often failed, I'd always wanted to do better, to be better. So shouldn't I at least be credited with a heroic defeat?

Satisfied with that summation, once again, I gave up and relinquished myself to a death that I hoped would be abrupt enough to be relatively painless.

However, at this point, I noticed a change—my movement seemed to have leveled out. I popped an eye open and saw I now drifted horizontally, carried by an easy current across a vast green plain. To my stunned surprise, I'd somehow made it through the perilous Clapping Mountains—they now lay behind me. In the distance ahead, I found a sky blue lake and seven geese swimming over its smooth surface in a single file line.

"Well, perhaps I judged my bride-to-be too harshly," I thought. I recalled her elegant reserve. Such grace would inspire me to a finer sensibility, a finer way of life. Yes, the father would not give her up so easily. But it was time for my beloved to leave the nest. I'm sure she'd realize it was for her own good and tell her father so. Or maybe we could sneak away in the night.

I lighted down on the shore by some reeds and watched the family as they paddled around—rather aimlessly, it seemed to me. Time and time again, they dipped their bills into the water without bringing anything up. Such a silly bunch.

"Oh, so you made it, son," the father said, rather flatly. "I guess we'll have to make you one of the family now."

"That's good, that's wonderful," I said. "When shall we have the ceremony? The sooner the better, I say."

"Indeed, it will be soon. Tomorrow, we continue south, traveling over the Slapping Mountains. When we arrive at the roost, you two can be married."

"Slapping Mountains?" I asked.

"Like the Clapping Mountains, but worse."

"Forget it," I told him. "She's not worth it."

Using my last flutter of strength, I then flew away from that family of fools. I was tired—physically tired, yes, but also tired in spirit. I was tired of myself. Tired of my self-deceiving ways. I needed some rest.

After I don't know how long, I awoke to find myself in the desert once more. What?—where was the green plain? Somehow I had jumped from one locale to another. No matter—at least, I didn't have to cross those damn Clapping Mountains again.

For the rest of the morning, I just wandered around while the heat slowly numbed my body and mind. I didn't know where to go or what to do. So I wandered.

Then, near midday, a thrumming sound broke against the wall of my stupor. A chirring—achingly-faint but growing stronger—touched my inner ear. I looked all about, but could not locate the source of the sound. It seemed to come from everywhere, from everything at once: from the rocks, the sun-burnt yellow grass, from the skeleton of a stunted tree.

That grinding vibration filled me; I become one with the sound, rising it rose, falling as it fell.

Within that frequency, I detected many separate entities of sound—individual sounds within the one big sound. I then realized I was also many in one—I could feel the particles of my being churn in harmony. I settled down to the ground, so I could lose myself in the sound completely—be consumed by it. I'd never felt such desire to totally surrender. Oh, the sweet agony! I thought I might soon die the dizzy death of the lover who loves too much—and I didn't care.

I broke from this meditation as the sound outside suddenly intensified. I thought my heart might burst from the drone of the buzzing.

Then the sound shut off abruptly. I stood there, confused by the loss, exhaling a sigh of relief, but also of sadness.

Just a short hop away lay a sun-bleached cow skull.

"Poor cow," I said to the skull, "did you die from the painful pleasures of that sound?"

In the silence that followed, I perceived a faint echo of that thrumming chirr coming from the inner recesses of the skull.

I peered into an empty eye socket, then winced as the vibration intensified for a moment and drummed against my eyeball.

Flummoxed, I was. How could a cow skull produce such a choir?

In the next instant, a stream of flies poured from the socket, circled me once, then reentered the skull through the opposite socket. Again, silence.

"Flies, my friends!" I said, speaking into the eye socket. "Tell me about that sound. It touches me to the core. It seems to reside inside this skull. Do you control it? I want to be filled fully with that song. If deprived, I think I might go mad."

"Well, then, come on in," the flies droned in unison. "The sound is an entity that lives deep within and only waits for you to wake it again."

"Flies, be serious," I whined. "I can't possibly fit in there!"

"Oh yes, you can—if we exit. Then there'll be enough room for your head."

The flies flowed out of the skull again and hovered quietly in a black cloud nearby. I didn't hesitate, but slipped my noggin through the hole at the base of the skull. Though the cow head felt a little snug, I could breathe well enough.

"You're right," I said. "It fits." My own voice sounded off the bone. "But where's that wonderful music? What do I do to wake it?"

"Sorry, but it left when we left," the flies buzzed in glee. "Because we are that sound. We merely used that skull as an amplifier." They erupted in razzing laughter!

"An ampli—"

But those deceitful flies didn't linger a moment longer. They wove their way through the air over the plain in a long snaky chain.

"Come back! Come back here! I demand you come back here right now." My voice rang inside the skull and pained my ears. Once again, my desire had led me astray.

Then began the work of trying to remove the cow skull from my poor raven head. I tugged. I pried. I twisted it this way and that, until fire lit up my spine.

Yet the skull remained clamped to my head, tight as a fist. I felt ridiculous.

The desert ground radiated a brutal heat. My mouth felt so parched—my tongue started to swell.

Wobbling from the bulky top weight, I stepped blindly until I finally managed to find a stream.

But blocked by the snout of the skull, I couldn't even get a sip of that shallow water. Unless I got this lid off quick, I'd die of thirst.

I sank into self-pity and sat down by the stream. I wept, caring not that I wasted precious fluids.

But soon my nostrils started to drip and since I couldn't wipe my beak dry, I decided to stand back up.

I then spotted two women drawing water from the stream a short distance away. Their fleshy brown arms had dimpled elbows. They chattered like sparrows, laughing and smiling—until they noticed me. Dropping their water jugs, they hid their faces behind their hands.

"Oh terrible monster," the women cried, "do not harm us. All we want is water for our village. Please spare our lives!"

"Be calm, my dear ones," I told them. "Though I'm a monster, I will not hurt you—as long as you do as I ask. Run to your village and fetch a sturdy mallet. Within my head is good medicine for your people. Medicine in the form of blessing. But in order to receive this medicinal blessing, you must break the head open. Don't worry—you won't kill me. All I ask is that your people bring some nice shiny trinkets in exchange."

My main concern was getting this damn skull off, but if I could make a little side-profit, then why not?

"Yes, we will do as you ask," the women replied, then turned and ran for their village, showing me the callused pads of their feet, light-brown with desert dust.

In short time, a cloud of that same color rose on the horizon. A line of people emerged from the cloud. When the villagers arrived at the stream, they laid their shiny trinkets of gold and silver and turquoise on the bank across from me.

"That's nice, but where's the mallet?"

The two women crossed the water and with a deep bow, set a mallet at my feet.

"Now bring your strongest warrior to me!" I commanded.

A young man approached. He minced his steps and held his head low in a show of fear and respect. His chest and abdomen gleamed with taut bands of muscle.

"What's your name?" I demanded.

"He Who Kills Birds," he whispered.

"Interesting name," I said. "Now, He Who Kills Birds, I hold some good medicine in this head of mine. But in order to get the blessing, you must take that mallet and give the crown a small tap. Just a soft stroke. Be gentle, for the sake of the medicine."

He Who Kills Birds then touched the mallet to the top of the skull. The force of that stroke, muted though it was, shot right through the cow bone and gave my brain a sharp sting. But the dry bone didn't even crack.

"Okay, okay," I told the warrior. "Try it again, but this time, put a little more into it."

He Who Kills Birds lifted the mallet to chin-level. In the next moment, hot lightning ripped down my spine. My brain began to throb against the cranium. Nonetheless, the cow skull remained intact. But with freedom so near, I was willing to endure even worse.

"Okay, alright, you're close. This time, put some muscle into it and be done!"

"But I don't want to hurt the medicine."

"Don't worry about that. It'll be okay. Just get on with the job."

The warrior raised the mallet over his head. I tensed my body and waited with dread.

The blast shot another lightning bolt down my spine. In the flash of an instant, my heart burst—an exploding volcano. Fire roared through my body. A rage of stinging teeth.

Through great force of will, I managed to settle a bit. I could feel the frayed flaps of my heart slapping around in the wind of the aftermath.

But no, that strike had not even cracked the skull. "Again," I rasped. "You want...this blessing...or not...you weak flea...inspire your muscles."

I opened my eyes a tiny fraction. The mallet head slowly rose until it seemed but a speck against the clouds. He Who Kills Birds suddenly took a big suck of air then gave a hard grunt—awrrrrrrrff!

Then the shadow of that hammer rushed down and in less than a breath, I shattered into fine insignificant dust.

I really didn't feel much—the gale wind resulting from that blow blew me past all extremities of pain. I spread in all directions at once and kept spreading until I finally reached the edges of the known Universe. For an infinite moment in space, I experienced perfect sighing peace.

Then all the tiny specks of me contracted simultaneously and zoomed back toward the center. When all that stuff slammed together in an instant, I became a dense rock. But the pressure did not stop; I kept compacting. Unable to endure the pain—an agony beyond burning—I finally abandoned that husk and floated freely, aimlessly—a wobbly bubble amid the emptiness of black space.

In the distance, I could hear sounds that matched the high-pitched warblings of a wildcat. After listening carefully, I recognized the voice of my own suffering.

Then nothing.

After I don't know how long, I awoke in a fog cloud. The gray clouds dispersed—too quickly, it seemed—and I found myself in a ragged, blasted body with a burnt brain. However, the realization that I was now free from that damn cow skull gave me strength enough to stand.

The skull, split neatly in half, lay on the ground. The villagers had dispersed, taking their trinkets with them. No, they no longer feared me—a monster with true power wouldn't be so fragile.

After filling my belly with cool stream water, I preened my feathers a bit, then continued on my way.

Again, I flew around aimlessly, asking myself questions, then forgetting those questions before I could answer them. I couldn't think. I didn't register what I saw or heard. I was only aware of some deep unnameable craving.

Finally something managed to break through my stuporous slump. A strange scent touched my raven nose. Though faint, it was bold; both burnt and fresh. It had the power of a dream. I could not resist—I followed the whisperings of that fragrance.

The landscape below quickly transformed. Burly sagebrush began to crowd the plain as the brown-white earth turned red-brown.

Spindly pines appeared on hillsides. Leafy trees crowded out those pines; those leafy trees became taller.

Suddenly, I spotted a clearing. In the center of the clearing, a circle of people sat around a campfire. People of all ages. They might be friend, they might be foe, but I hardly cared—the scent had hooked my nose and I gladly that hook pull me down to their campfire.

I settled to the ground and with a flourish of my wings, bowed to the tribe. The burnt-but-fresh scent nearly overpowered me now.

An old woman approached me. She had swollen knees and legs with large blue veins.

"Hello, Grandmother," I said.

"Welcome, Raven," she said. "What brings you to us?"

"A wonderful fragrance guided me here. A scent that rules my heart. My desire to discover its source negates all other desires. What do you do that creates such a delicious smell?"

"That must be the acorn cakes. Would you care to join us?"

"Certainly."

I followed the old woman to a place near the fire. I sat down and two young maidens then presented me with a stack of steaming-hot acorn cakes.

In my eagerness, I scorched my tongue on the first one. Ah, but as soon as that cake landed in my stomach, it rekindled the fire that I'd lost.

To stoke that flame, I gobbled up those cakes and begged for more.

The tribespeople smiled all around, pleased by my pleasure. For the moment at least, my belief in the goodness of life was restored.

After three more stacks, my stomach felt happily bloated. I squelched a big belch, then addressed the maidens. "Tell me, my dears, how do you make those magical cakes? I know it must be your most valued secret. But if you can tell me, please do."

"It is no secret, Raven," said the maidens, speaking as one, their notes clear and round. "You just mix some ground-up acorns into moist flour, press that mix into small cakes, then shove the cakes under a fire."

"Maidens, dear maidens," I protested, "don't tease me. Please tell the truth. Nothing so grand could be so simple. If you can't share the secret, just say so."

"But beautiful Raven, we have told you the truth!"

"I'll believe the truth when I hear it." Were they laughing at me beneath their lovely smiles? My anger started to rise.

Fortunately, at this point, the old woman with blue-veined legs motioned the maidens over and whispered to them. The two just shrugged, then walked back to me.

"Okay, Raven," they sighed, "we will tell you the secret."

Following the maidens' instructions, I then gathered the largest, shiniest acorns from the oldest oak tree in the forest.   Only the unblemished were acceptable.

This task took the rest of the morning and part of the afternoon, but my desire gave me patience. I then loaded the acorns into a canoe and began to paddle my way toward the bend in the river described by the maidens: a place where the water churned with a wicked ferocity.

I'd been told to dump the acorns overboard there, so they could soak and soften.   According to the maidens, the spiraling current would suck them down to the bottom of the river.

They'd given me a small walnut-tree branch. I was to count every leaf on that branch, then dive overboard and retrieve all the acorns—not one should be left behind. Afterwards, I would squash them up using only my right foot.

Then I'd make the flour by grinding maize—and of course, the grain must be polished first.

Only then would the maidens help me mix the acorn cakes. After that, we'd recite a special prayer and place the cakes into the fire.

As I neared the bend, the river began to snarl and whip its many tails. The rapids foamed over the sides of the canoe, drenching my feathers as I dumped the acorns into the water.

Unfortunately, most of them floated away with the current. But I decided to remain true to the project. While still working the canoe paddle, I counted the leaves as quickly as possible, then took a deep breath and ignoring instinct, dove into the brutally-cold water in hopes of finding what few acorns rested on the bottom.

I woke to find myself spread out on the ground with the Grandmother squeezing down on my chest. Rough water jagged up from my lungs and squirted out my beak. "Did I get any of the acorns?" I coughed. "Did they soak long enough?"

"You disappoint us, Raven," said she of the swollen knees. "But I guess even the cleverest among us has an occasional lapse of judgment. Desire can mislead even the strong."

"That has been my experience," I told her.

Two young warriors then lifted me up and set me down by the fire to dry. For the rest of the evening, the maidens fed me those scorching-hot acorn cakes— which are made from whatever acorns you may find on the ground, just as long as they're not rotten. And of course, you don't have to squash them with your right foot. But you do need to pick the bugs out.

A simple concoction; an exquisite pleasure.

When I woke the next morning, somehow I knew I was done here—though it pained me to leave this generous tribe. I didn't know where I needed to go, I only knew I needed to go.

Before I left, I thanked the tribespeople for their kindness. And they, in turn, thanked me for blessing them with my presence. Then I took wing again, following the wind and never pausing long enough to allow myself to think too deeply.

The tribe had provided me with a brief warm respite. But in mind and heart, I was still a mess.

I remember nothing more of that day except the easy green blur of the trees below me.

I woke the next morning to find myself perched on a flat rock, deep in a cool shadowy forest. The wind occasionally ssshed through the trees, whipping water from leaves, exploding the quiet as the drops splattered down.

I felt the urge to continue my aimless traveling. But a stronger compulsion kept me waiting on the rock. Not until the late afternoon sunlight angled through the trees, did I discover the reason behind this intuition.

First, I heard the scraping of feet through dry leaves. Then I spotted a young man with a slain deer slung across his shoulders. As he stopped for a breath near the flat rock, an idea suddenly came to me.

"Excuse me," I said.

"What? Who's there? Show yourself!" He raised his bow and looked all around.

"Down here. On the rock. It's me—Raven."

He jumped back, then blinked and blinked and blinked his eyes—trying to believe what he was seeing and hearing.

"What—what what do you want from me?" The words nearly stuck in his throat.

"I'll tell you what I want: that deer you've got there. Give me the deer and I will tell you a story."

"No, I can not give you the deer," the warrior said. "My name is He Who Brings Home Deer. Though young, I am a hunter of great prowess. Whenever I hunt, I never fail to bring a deer home to my mother. She relies on me. Besides, I have my reputation to protect."

Blood dripped from the deer's snout. I could already taste that sweet, salty paste on my tongue.

"Put the deer down," I said, "and listen to my story." I could see that He Who Brings Home Deer had a hungry mind and hungry spirit. He not only wanted my story, he *needed* my story. And that deer seemed to me to be just what I needed to put my life right. "Lay the deer down. Your life requires this tale."

Finally, He Who Brings Home Deer bowed to his higher will and flopped the deer down beside me. Blood oozed from the nostrils and pooled on the rock.

I then told the young warrior how the great Creator had given Raven a spin and as Raven spun what he'd once seen as one, but he now saw as many. In this way, all the creatures came into being. Partly for the benefit of humans—to provide food, yes, but also so people could learn from them and know the right way to live.

I told him Raven had lifted the moon and sun into the sky; Raven had slung the stars across the night and spread the seas and rivers upon the land.

"Yes," I said, opening my wings wide, "I have done much for you and your kind."

At that moment, I spied two older warriors listening from behind two trees.

Before I could speak, they leapt into the clearing and shouted, "What goes on here! He's telling you lies. Coyote actually did what Raven claims to have done."

"Wrong wrong, totally wrong, whoever you are. I'm here, right now, and I'm telling you the truth."

He Who Brings Home Deer met their glare with a glare of this own. "I believe Raven," he said defiantly.

"You want to know who I am? I am He Who Shoulders Life," one of the older warriors said. This man wore a heavy brow. In his eyes I saw dark suspicion. "I heard you claim you threw the sun and moon and stars into the sky. Well, maybe so, but you didn't say how."

"Yeah," his comrade said. "You didn't say say how."

"Okay," I answered. "Prepare to be amazed."

Perhaps you're expecting me to now retell the story of how Raven got Gull to release the light. Well, that did happen, but the story below also happened:

Long long ago, I looked down from a hole in the sky and saw human beings stumbling about in the dark, unable to hunt or fish properly, tripping over and bumping into each other and growing angry and striking at one another and cursing and urinating on and defecating on anything that got in their way.

I knew I must help them. So I lowered myself down and let the wind guide me across the dark plain and through the woods until I arrived at a cabin with soft golden light spreading out from its front door—the cabin where The Man Who Kept Light lived. How did I know he lived there? I just knew.

"How can I get at his light?" I wondered. "How can I infiltrate that dwelling?"

In the next moment, I received my answer when the daughter of The Man Who Kept Light stepped out to draw water from a nearby stream.

I then shrank myself to the size of a dust mote and drifted down onto the water and let her scoop me up in her bucket. Then when she tipped the bucket to take a drink, I slipped right down her gullet.

"Oh, I felt secure in the warm dark red of her belly. The blood pulsations calmed me with their measured repetition and I eased into a deep, rich sleep. In that blessed state, I dreamt a dream that told me everything about everything, which of course, I forgot as soon as I awoke, because I awoke to find myself hanging from the hand of a midwife, being whacked to life—a new-born human baby.

In that way, I became part of The Man Who Kept Light's family. They loved me and fed me and let me have the run of the place. Under these propitious conditions, I shot up like a corn sprout soaked with spring rain. Everyone whooped with amazement as my legs and arms and trunk grew up and out before their very eyes.

But then, following my plan, I began to wail at the top of my lungs. Every day, all day long, and every night, all night long, I wailed. Finally, The Man Who Kept Light told his daughter, "Take that bag down from the wall and let him play with it. Maybe then he'll shut up."

After they gave me that glowing bag, I rolled it back and forth over the floor, just like any baby would. But as soon as the family turned their backs, I let the bag go and it floated straight up to the ceiling and then out through the smoke hole and then shot to the top of the sky. The bag opened then and all the stars flew out and the wind scattered those silvery jewels across the black heavens.

Finally, the humans of the earth had some light. But not nearly enough, of course. So I shrieked and hollered and yelled some more. In short time, The Man Who Kept Light told his daughter, "Take that other bag from the wall. Let him play with it. If he doesn't shut up soon, we'll have to drown him."

This second bag glowed through the cloth even more than the first. As before, I rolled it back and forth across the room just like any healthy baby would. But when the family went outside, I let the bag go. As with the first, it squeezed up through the smoke hole, then leapt into the sky. When the bag opened, the moon popped out and cut a round hole in the starry darkness.

So people then had the light of the moon and the light of the stars. But they still needed more light. Though my vocal cords now stung from previous work, I continued to scream and yell. Soon, The Man Who Kept Light said to his daughter, "Take that last bag off the wall and give it to your son before I devour him whole."

The third bag was the biggest and brightest bag of all. It radiated a suffocating heat. So, I didn't waste any time—I released it instantly. But due to its size, the bag got stuck in the smoke hole. What could I do? I needed to get out of that house before the father acted on his violent urges. So with a quick whirl, I threw off my baby body. Then I unfurled my raven wings and flew up to the hole.

But though I threw all my weight against that bag, I could not shove it through. The family, once so loving, began cursing and throwing household objects at me.

As I continued to push, the father worked furiously to fan up a big fire and as the thick smoke clawed into my lungs, I hacked with a fit of coughing, yet at the same time, went giddy as my blood began to boil and percolate up into my head.

Yes, the heat grew more and more intense and the air kept expanding. The cabin began to shiver, then began to shake, and shook until boards began to groan and crack. Finally the house broke free and ascended into the sky with me still stuck at the smoke hole.

My stomach fell down and down and cold air filled my empty gut as the cabin shot up into the heavens.

When the roof hit the top of the sky, all those rickety boards and shingles burst into splinters.

Then with one quick tug of my beak, I whipped off the tie cord and the sun leapt from the bag.

"And that, my friends, is why you have the sun's life-giving light today. My gift to you, at great risk to my own safety." I felt quite pleased with my narrative, but when I saw the wide puzzled eyes of the three hunters, I realized the tale needed some explanation in order to be credible.

But the question asked was not the question I'd expected.

"So they lived in houses then?" He Who Shoulders Life asked me.

"Yes, they lived in houses then. Or some such dwelling."

With that, the hunters seemed satisfied. In fact, they wanted to hear more. But I said they must wait until the following day—when they should bring the entire tribe.

Though I'd told a whooping tale, I assured myself it indeed held truth. That truth is in the answer to the question I'd expected but not received.   And that answer is this:

"I know you may be wondering why The Man Who Kept Light and his daughter acted so foolishly. I mean, why let a baby play with your precious bags of light? Well, I believe: that family did what they did because the world needed them to do what they did.

"I say: we sometimes need to be the fools we are."

The next afternoon, all the people of the tribe followed the three hunters into the clearing. Their eyes shone with wonder as they gazed upon me. After the hunters piled fresh carrion beside my rock, the tribespeople settled in, then waited for my story with intense expectation.

I wasted no time, but drew a great breath, then told them about my remarkable journey, a journey that began with with a bold solo trip into The Land of the Dead.   I told how I'd escaped a mad boulder that wanted my blanket, how I'd courageously crossed the perilous Clapping Mountains, how I'd defeated He Who Kills Birds despite his mighty mallet, and finally, how I'd celebrated with a tribe after making them a great delicacy known as acorn cakes.

When I'd finished, the tribespeople approached me humbly in ones and twos, and thanked me for my stories. Mothers and fathers asked me to bless their babies.

Okay, so I exaggerated a little in the telling. The important thing is: I gave the tribe some Raven tales that would feed their hungry spirits for seasons without number.

Standing on my rock, I opened my wings to them all and said, "Carry these stories with you always, to tell and retell until people everywhere know of Raven and are that much wiser for the knowing."

I then seemed to leap forward in time.

I suddenly found myself flying high above the trees again. I didn't remember leaving the clearing. What'd happened to all that good carrion? Had I dreamt the entire scene?

Whatever the reality was, I felt a sense of completion. But what had I completed? Could I finally leave this strange land? Would I now find a home?

I flew around for I don't know how long, hoping to discover the door to some type of deliverance. Yes, I thought I'd learned something through my travels. Nonetheless, I was still a lost bird.

And so, when I spotted another encampment of humans, I decided to plunk myself right down. "Maybe instead of chasing life, I should let life come to me," I said. "No more searching."

This peaceful tribe welcomed me immediately. They fed me. They listened to me. They treated me with diffidence and respect. I quickly settled in. As the moon went from lean to full, I conversed with these people and hunted and fished with them and, in general, took all the pleasure life offered.

Then one day, as I sat by a stream watching the water twist shadow and light, a strange warrior emerged from the trees. His face was a nightmare mask. Those eyes glinted with cool silver malice. That down-turned mouth signaled unhappiness and cruelty. His tall frame moved with a wide conquering stride.

The tribespeople all stood stone-quiet as he entered their modest village. He approached a young woman hanging fish on a line to dry. "Those are mine now," he told her.

Without hesitation, she picked the fish off the line and put them in a basket for him. The warrior then left, quite at his ease.

"Why'd you give that man those fish?" I asked the woman. "You need them to feed your family."

"You don't know him," she said. "He's the one we all fear. Every breath he breathes is evil. Every step he takes is evil. Every muscle in his body is saturated with evil. He is evil evil evil."

"So what's his name?"

"We call him The One with Bad Manners," she replied.

"I suddenly see what I must do. I now know the purpose behind my being here. I must kill The One with Bad Manners. Then I will be done."

During my respite, I'd had a chance to reflect on my journey. Yes, I'd met many challenges and endured, but I hadn't exactly triumphed. I now wanted to show myself I could be more than I'd been.

A young warrior named Dark Eyes approached me. Storm clouds weighed upon his brow. "No one dares fight The One with Bad Manners," he said, shaking his head.

"But *I* will," I said.

"You don't understand. He has a grandmother even more evil than he is. And she has provided a guardian for him—a bear, and not just any bear either. A bear so massive and powerful that it can switch the course of a river with one swipe of its paw. A bear that can blow trees into splinters with its roar. Don't mess with that bear, Raven, unless you want trouble. My brother, leave The One with Bad Manners alone."

"Well," I said to myself, "maybe he doesn't invade their turf on a regular basis...but no, I have already made my statement, I have taken on this responsibility, I have set the act in motion. I must continue through to the end."

"Sorry, but you can not deter me, my brother," I told Dark Eyes. "Just bring me some arrows and a stout bow."

The days grew short and the shadows became cold as I hunted over the land for the evil warrior. I did not sleep nor eat for more days than I can remember. I had a purpose beyond myself and felt secure in my mission, in my obedience to a higher will.

Finally one afternoon, fortune led me to a stream where The One with Bad Manners had knelt down to drink. I dropped to the bank across from him, stared into his cool silvery eyes, and said, "I have come here to kill you and do away with all the evil in the world."

The One with Bad Manners merely lifted his upper lip and sneered at me with black rotten teeth.

He waved his hand over his head. A dark lumbering shape, great in bulk, moved among the trees behind him. Shank and shoulder muscle rolled under heavy fur.

That black mountain of a bear paused at the edge of the wood. The beast was as silent and as still as the breath of death in winter. I waited with the patience of a rock.

Then time snapped forward: the bear sprang from the trees, rearing up on its hind legs before me. It had the height and girth of an ancient oak. A roar rumbled up from the canyon of its belly, using forth with a wind that shook the trees and tore away leaves. Saliva dropped from its chin, hitting my head with heavy globs—I had to blink my eyes clear.

And yet, I stood fast. My talons anchored me to the spot.

The bear stared down at me, squinching up its small dumb eyes, puzzled by my equanimity. I simply smiled back.

Determined to knock that grin off my face, the bear lifted its paw. The curved claws glinted like ice in the sun.

But I was ready and pulled back my bowstring.

The fat paw halted in mid-flight. My arrow had struck the beast squarely in the chest. Those tiny eyes froze in abject confusion.

The bear then began folding in upon itself, quickly collapsing inside. Thick furry skin piled upon thick furry skin in softly-rounded layers. Soon, that bear was no more than a big hairy mound on the ground.

The One with Bad Manners stared at the mound for a moment, then turned his sharp, silver malice back to me. In a single motion, displaying both power and grace, I drew back my bowstring and split the distance between his eyebrows with an arrow.

The eyes widened in disbelief. Their evil light died down the dark wells of those pupils. The One with Bad Manners flopped forward like a felled tree.

As I left that scene, I strode through the forest with great assurance. I felt that I, I alone, commanded these woods. I was Raven, master of the Earth

According to destiny's design, my path led me straight to a cabin. I knew, without being told, who dwelled within. The grandmother. Stronger and more evil than her grandson and his bear combined. But I did not hesitate, I did not falter; no, I pounded on the door and yelled, "Come out, old woman! I have killed your grandson as well as his guardian bear and now, I must kill you, because you're responsible for them—for all the evil they'd done in the world."

"Oh, so it's Raven, huh?" that crusty old-gal croaked from behind her wooden door. "Well, I won't come out. Not for you. Not unless I want to, and I don't."

"Come on, old woman!" I cried. "Anyone as evil as you can't resist a good fight."

"You act brave now," she said, "but if you took off your Raven mask and your Raven wings and that Raven skin and those Raven feet, you wouldn't feel so sure of yourself."

"That's absurd," I said. "I can't be other than what I am and I am Raven."

"But if you took off your Raven mask and your Raven wings and feet and skin, you wouldn't be Raven anymore. You would be a man, just an ordinary human man. And as a man, you would be helpless against me."

"I know what I am—I am Raven, not man."

"Take off your Raven mask, then you will see what you really are."

What could I say? What could I do? She had challenged my identity. And I had failed to answer her charge.

Well, just to shut the old hag up, I decided to attempt the impossible. I sat down on the ground, grabbed my beak with my claws and gently tugged.

Lo and behold, a feather helmet lifted right off my head. I then slung the wings from my arms, then stood and let the Raven skin slip from my body. All that remained were my Raven feet. But I decided to let them be.

Just to be sure of my transformation, I touched my human nose, felt my human chest, and ran my tongue over my human teeth. A strange revelation indeed! But I had no time to consider its implications.

"Okay, Granny," I said, "right now, I am indeed a man. But just as strong as before. So come on out and defend yourself. I am ready to rid the world of you."

I stepped back four paces.

The cabin shuddered with the force of the old woman's indignation. Suddenly, the door burst from its frame and flew through the air. In the next moment, the flimsy boards of that shack burst asunder in a shower of splinters that made me wince.

As my eyes cleared, I found before me a figure much larger than the dwelling that'd held it. Feet resembling boulders led up to knobbled legs with blue snaky veins. The agitated tentacles of her crotch hair groped the air and her pleated breasts drooped with the boredom of ghosts long dead. She had a face that matched the hacked and craggy features of a weather-beaten cliff. Smoke leaked from enlarged nostrils. Her enormous head blocked the sun.

"Poor, poor Raven!" she cried with a voice like the screeching wind. "I see you're not so brave now without your Raven clothes."

I didn't want to admit it, but she was right. My legs shook so hard that my teeth rattled. I felt like running, but couldn't move my feet. A weak, pink feeling in my gut spread throughout my body.

I tried to find a little bit of strength within. But my mind began to swirl, to whirl down, drawn by the vacuum of a bottomless pit.

When I managed focus again, I saw dark gray clouds spiraling around the old woman's towering frame. Soon, she was completely hidden inside a muscular massive cloud.

Then a blaze of lightening ripped down and through the cloud and broke that formation into small tufts. Where the hag had stood, I now found a monstrous purple snake, its skin marked by a crisscross pattern of black lines. The long body stood vertical. Its head was as high as the trees.

A shocking vision that spurred me to an act of self-preservation. Summoning what remained of my gumption, I managed to brace my trembling body and raise my bow and aim my arrow.

Such disappointment then, as that arrow drifted softly through the air and dinged off the iron-hard skin without causing even a fraction of harm.

The jaws of the beast now swung open and the crimson mouth began descend toward me. Its silver teeth were so sharp that my eyes stung.

"Sssseeee, I told you. You have no power without your Raven clothessssss," the old woman-snake hissed at me. "As a man, you can not defeat me."

I wilted into my inner self as my bones liquefied. Not wishing to face my humiliation, I gave up my sight.

I waited for the crunch of death, hoping the pain wouldn't be too severe.

But then, down deep in the dark, I began to sense a force building—an unknown yet undeniable strength. Suddenly this force surged forward and became my will. Working against my fearful objections, it made my limbs strong again; it made me open my eyes and look up.

Though I still shivered with fear, I again lifted my bow, I again aimed my arrow. This time, the arrow tore like lightning-fire through the air and straight into that crimson trap. It slipped between the two long fangs, entered the roof of the mouth, then exited, neatly at the top of the head.

With a "pop" and a long downward whistle, the snake deflated in a moment. The empty purple hide slapped the ground and soon faded to a mere shadow.

"Yes, old woman," I said to the shadow, "as a man I knew weakness, but only then could I find true courage. Only then could I—"

"Oh shut up!" the grandmother croaked.

And with that, her shadow disappeared into the earth.

Despite my triumph as a man, I was anxious to regain my former identity. So I did not wait but put my Raven outfit back on and then began to fly again. But I wouldn't return to the tribe. I knew I was done there.

I didn't care about direction or destination. That's not to say I flew aimlessly—my "aim" was to keep on going. I'd decided that wherever I went was where I needed to be. So I wasn't lost. This belief served me well—it eased my worry.

And maybe that decision freed me—because I soon came to the canyon where the shamans-in-training resided.

The three neophytes still stood at the same cliff edge, still strained to "see".

I dove into the scraggly trees and sagebrush below the cliff and took a drink from the spring. In short time, Ruficollis, Quork, and Squee settled down beside me.

"So, I see you finally made it back," the swaggering, bow-legged Rufi said.

"We were starting to become concerned," Quork said.

I narrowed my eyes at that oddball Squee. "Someone ditched me out there. You can't imagine all I've endured."

"Please tell us," Quork said. "Please do." His pleading tones made a mockery of his affected sophistication.

"I looked around and you weren't there," Squee

claimed. "I wanted to wait, but couldn't."

"Well, I can't say I blame you for being in a hurry. A strange place, The Land of Tales. I did things there I'm embarrassed to mention. Silly stuff—crazy. Like I was possessed."

"In The Land of Tales you reenact the stories of Raven," Quork said. "So many stories in that land, stories that have existed since time began."

"I only went through a few, but that was enough."

"You live the ones crucial to your education at a particular time."

"I seemed to lack free will," I told them. "I made decisions, yeah. But I wasn't really thinking."

"In The Land of Tales you make the mistakes you need to make in order to learn what you need to learn," Quork said.

"Well, actually I feel dumber, not smarter now. But anyway, why haven't I heard of The Land of Tales before?"

"The Land is one of our little secrets," Squee said. "Known only to shamans and shamans-in-training. Yes, we do tell those tales to our flocks. But we dare not reveal there's a place where they could relive the tales. Don't want them to waste their time trying to get there. And if someone did manage to slip in, well, easy to get confused if you don't know what you're doing. Could ruin the mind of even the strongest."

"Well, I got confused, but fortunately, I wasn't ruined. You should have given me a little more information."

"Eventually, every shaman-in-training must go there. Usually more than once before he graduates," Quork said, ignoring my complaint. "That's how we grow so wise in such a short time. The experience is more intense than day-to-day living, so our learning is accelerated."

"But enough about that," Rufi hoarsed. "We want some information. Tell us what happened over there!"

"Let me talk to your shaman first," I said. This time I'd demand he speak to me.

The would-be shamans looked down and shuffled their feet in the dust. "Well, ah, actually, we haven't seen him for some time. Since you were last here," Squee said. "We haven't been summoned to his cave."

"The old bird could be dead for all you know!" I shouted.

The trio just stood there, studying their toes. Those guys were really starting to wear on my patience. I took another drink from the spring to help cool myself down. I needed to clear the desert heat from my head.

"Any raven able to go into The Land of Tales must surely be destined for shaman-hood," Quork said, then added delicately, "You still won't tell us what happened?"

"Find out about it on your own!"

"We're probably not quite ready," Quork and Rufi chorused.

Well, I couldn't argue with that statement.

Without waiting a moment more, I shot up through the trees and began making my way across the canyon—quite relieved to be done with those fools. Now more than ever, I was determined not to enter the trade of shamanism. Many questions occurred to me.

If you could learn so much in The Land of Tales, why was their shaman such a dull crow? For that matter, I doubted going into that land could ever completely cure that trio of their silliness—no matter how often they went. But who was I to criticize? I'd felt like an idiot before venturing into The Land, and I still felt like one afterwards—though maybe not quite as big of an idiot. I realized then The Land of Tales could facilitate my learning, but it was up to me to see what I was trying to learn.

After feeling a rush of freedom, I began to quiet down. I spread my wings allowed myself to coast as much as possible. I'd been through so much in what now seemed a short time. I suppose I should have felt exultant—to have experienced such a wild, weird, wonderful kaleidoscope and emerged alive and somewhat intact. Maybe I had indeed gained wisdom. Nonetheless, I had to admit: I still felt lost. Maybe wherever I went was where I needed to be, *but I still felt lost*. And that feeling diminished my sense of accomplishment.

"Okay, maybe I *needed* to be in this desert," I said to myself. "But after all that's happened, I think I must be done here." To my mind, this dry land represent hardship, uncertainty, loss. But I dared not become too distraught. I might very well find myself trapped here by the inner force of my higher will. Stuck here 'til the end of my days.

In any case, the flat plain seemed endless on all four sides of me.

That evening, I settled in under a broken boulder. A bitter wind slipped through the cracks and snuck under my feathers until my whole body shook with the cold.

The next morning, as sunlight splintered on the horizon, I detected an odd scent drifting on the wind. So very faint, but to my sensitive raven nose, also very rich. A stinging, multi-faceted smell. It spoke of magnificence—but also of brutality.

No question: I had to find the source of that scent.

Following its thread, I soon came to a mountainous region. Then after a short distance, the mountains smoothed to become hills filled with a panoply of trees, dazzling my eyes with so many shades of green.

Then the hills flattened. The forest ended. A pink sunset stained a ribbon of sand. I'd found the source. Here were the waters that spread all the way to the horizon. Though I'd heard tell of this liquid land, I'd never really believed the stories. Again and again, foaming waves claimed the beach, then sank back with exhaustion. The dark blue ocean heaved and slumped; celebrated and capitulated. I wanted to dive in and douse and dose myself with its great energy—I'd gladly be tossed like a twig by that indomitable force.

But as soon as I settled my feet on the beach, fatigue overtook me. I sheltered myself against the cold hard wind in the cranny of a rock and quickly fell asleep.

I awoke in the morning with a hunger that had me dancing in circles. What edibles existed in my new locale? I needed replenishing.

Looking out over the ocean, I found my answer. I kept seeing seagulls take nose-dives into the water and spring back out with squirming fish clamped in their beaks. If those ungainly birds, with their awkward floppy wings, could perform such a trick, why couldn't I?

But after several attempts, I'd only managed to spear a tiny minnow. By that time, my feathers were soggy wet and I felt a chill to my marrow. I hopped up and down on the sand, famished and freezing, watching those stupid gulls make catch after catch. How humiliating.

Then I saw something which, in my feeble-minded state, seemed to me to be the answer to my woes. In the far distance, a small flat island of shiny blue rose from the water. This isle floated on the ocean's surface for a few moments, then vanished beneath the waves. I waited. Several beats later, it resurfaced in a new location.

When the island again submerged, a big fish tail flopped out of the water and smacked the waves hard. The spray sang up whitely through the wind.

"That must be the massive creature known as Whale," I told myself.

Again, that island of lard rose up. The juices flowed under my tongue as I watched the whale rest bloatedly, half-buried in ocean water. Such a behemoth surely wouldn't miss a little chunk of flesh here or there, now would it?

At this point, I wish to state that ravens rarely feast on live animals. Generally, we say: live and let live. But I needed a meal and that whale had plenty of extra meat. I would not be stealing, I'd be redistributing wealth.

I winged out over the water, but the leviathan dove beneath the waves before I could land. However, its form was faintly visible beneath the blue. So when the whale resurfaced, I was waiting and plucked right down on its back.

I tested the flesh with my sharp beak. The tough hide gave, but did not break. I poked at the whale skin again and again, but my beak could not penetrate. Finally, I pressed my nose into the hide using all my weight and strength. Still no luck.

Let it be known that despite its enormous bulk, the whale is a sensitive creature. As I continued to try to drill into the flesh, the back began to ripple with spasms. The tail swung this way and that. Intent on my goal, I did not heed these warnings, but instead started jabbing like a woodpecker.

At last, a jot of blood slipped into my beak. But at the very moment of my triumph, the beast flipped its tail up, grazing my shoulder and knocking me sideways.

Those great gaping jaws rose out of the water. Still off balance and unable to get enough air under my wings, I fell spinning into the mouth of the beast.

The whale slapped back down on the water and as the jaws closed, I landed on the slab of its tongue. Before I could regain my feet, a blast of water hit me and carried me down to the bottom of a black pit. Plumes of sulfurous gases swarmed me. I could hear the muffled roar of the sea outside.

For too long, I waded around in the dark, searching for a way that would lead me up the throat. But I kept bumping into the smooth, tough walls of the whale's stomach. I dared not venture too far, lest I discover the wrong orifice.

I was angry at this creature, but even more angry at myself. Confusion and frustration returned to consume my mind. I was supposed to be a wiser bird now. But I felt like a joke. To make matters worse, I was still hungry.

Finally, I gave up, sat down in this black abyss, and wept.

"Well, at least my misery won't last long," I said to myself, "this place will kill me soon enough."

But then, through the darkness and the stench, my bleary eyes discerned a distant glow. I crawled toward that light, hoping for some type of deliverance.

What did I find but a small oil lamp on the floor. At regular intervals, a drop of oil would fall from the ribbed archway of the ceiling and land in a little round pool that fed the lamp.

By impulse, I lowered the tip of my wing toward the flame. But at that moment, a form appeared from out of the shadows: a coil of soft light slowly rotating, suspended in the air. I perceived a certain consciousness emanating from that spiral of nine rings. I understood that a being stood before me—a being more spirit than physical substance. It radiated a profound gentleness.

"Please do not touch the flame...please do not touch the lamp," the being said. Such a gentle warm tone.

"It looks so perfectly beautiful," I said. "But no worry—I just want to get out of here. Can you help me?"

"You will leave when you are ready to leave—"

"I assure you, I am ready."

"You are hungry."

"Oh yes."

"My name is Kapok. I live in this whale. Wait here. I will bring you fish. There's enough fish for both you and the whale. Wait here. But please, do not touch the lamp."

The wispy being of light then disappeared back into the shadows. A few moments later, it reappeared with a basket of fish suspended within its spiral.

Those coils abruptly dispersed and the basket fell to the floor.

Though I wondered what'd happened to Kapok, I did not wait, but immediately started in on those lovely fish, sucking them down my gullet, one after the other. Soon, my stomach was plumped-up beyond all reasonable parameter. In this condition, I fell back on my tail and went into a deep sleep.

When I awoke, the spiral of light had reformed and again hovered near me.

"Okay, I think I'm ready to go now," I said. "I assume you know a way out."

"I can get more fish."

Though I still felt full, the memory of my hunger lingered and so I said, "Okay, yeah, sure. More fish. Then I'll go."

"Wait here. But please, do not touch the lamp—

not even its flame."

"Okay, whatever. I don't want to burn myself."

"If you touched the lamp, it would be bad for the whale and bad for you as well."

"I said I wouldn't touch the lamp and I won't."

Kapok soon returned with another basket of fish. One after the other, those fish slid down my gullet and brought happiness to a stomach too sad for too long.

When I had finished, Kapok began to ask me about my life. I told her the whole mess, starting with my youth and its deep feeling of isolation, continuing with the battle between the flocks, then describing my wild flight through The Land of Tales and ending with my recent near-starvation. I must admit I omitted the part about trying to poke a hole in the whale. But overall, this narrative was much more honest than the version I'd shared with the tribe of He Who Brings Home Deer. Perhaps that's why I now felt a sense of release.

Kapok then spoke of her own life. She had tended to whales for as long as she could remember. Yes, on a basic level, a whale knows how to be a whale. But it needs some help when dealing with life's deeper dilemmas.

"So how do you communicate with the whale?" I asked.

"When the whale struggles with a difficult problem, it may go within—listen within—deep within, until it hears my voice."

"And then you give it the answer?"

"No. I can only provide the loving comfort of my being. But that love helps soothe the whale and bolster its strength."

"That's what I need," I thought to myself. "An inner Kapok. Why should whales be so lucky?" Now, I wasn't so eager to leave. I wanted some of that soothing love for myself.

Nonetheless, I felt a little irritated about the oil lamp. Why couldn't I touch it? What was so special about that lamp? I wanted to ask Kapok, but thought she might get suspicious about my intentions and ask me to leave. Well, yes, I still wanted to leave. But not until I'd discovered the secret behind that lamp. With each drop of oil, the mystery heightened—a small but incessant torture.

When Kapok again went to fetch fish, I turned my full attention to the gently-burning oil lamp. Though she had warned me—you could say "nagged" me—about touching either the lamp or its flame, she hadn't mentioned anything about the oil that fell from the ceiling. Perhaps I could satisfy my curiosity by testing the oil.

So I lifted my break and let the next drop land right in my mouth.

To my surprise, that bit of oil sang through my whole being like the honeyed milk of a soft full moon. A warm starry night sky unfurled in my mind. What bliss!

I'd barely recovered from this ecstasy when Kapok returned with another basket of fish. I gulped them down, just as before, but this time when I finished, I immediately asked for another basket. I could not wait —I had to have more of that wonderful oil.

As soon as she'd disappeared into the dark, I caught a second drop in my beak.

In an instant, I went into a dream world filled with a chorus of raven song, a myriad of calls blended into one. Yet even that wasn't enough for me: I wanted to go higher. I let another drop fall into my craw, then another and another.

I barely managed to stop before Kapok came back. But then I had to brace my feet in order to hold myself steady on the floor. I feared she'd say something. But no!—she merely twirled in the air as I stuffed that load of fish down my throat.

"Another basket," I managed to mutter. What a bloated belly! But so what if I got sick? I suffer anything for one more drop of oil. The lamp continued to burn with a steady glow, so obviously it didn't need the extra fuel.

This time, after Kapok left, I dispensed with all niceties and flew straight to top of the arched ribway, to the small hole that dripped the oil. I now ripped at the skin around that opening, hoping to make the oil flow more freely. Yes, Kapok might banish me, but I'd be well-saturated.

Occasionally, I'd pause in my work and allow another golden drop to slide down my gullet. As these drops bloomed within me, I lost myself completely—stabbing and tearing with my beak.

But in my frenzy, I forgot what a sensitive creature the beastly whale was. Soon, a booming wind roared down the canyon of the belly. The leviathan then began to roll from side to side. But I just dug my talons into the ceiling and held fast.

Finally—*finally!*—the oil shot out in a torrent. But at the same moment, the whale dove straight down. Even so, I kept my grip and managed to catch much of gushing oil in my mouth.

When the beast had reached the deepest depth of the deep, it turned and rocketed right back up, racing for the surface.

Crazed by mindless intoxication, I finally lost my hold. I flapped my wings, but had no control and so I bounced off the floor, then hit one wall, then the other, then ricocheted back to ceiling, and on and on: floor wall ceiling wall floor. Yet in all this tumult, I still felt the giddiness of my oil buzz.

As for the lamp, all the commotion knocked it off the floor; then it jiggled through the air, its light trailing behind like a golden fox tail. I tried to nab it again and again, but in the clumsiness of my high, only chipped my beak.

As the whale accelerated its ascent, I heard a long screaming raven cry. From where?—from me, that's where: from the depths of my bowels. My body would surely explode from forces both external and internal. But maybe a good way to go—having reached the highest high, I would end my story by bursting like a falling star, a spectacular spectacle—an empty glory, yes, but dramatic in its emptiness. I'd die unknown, unmourned, forgotten—*just desserts*, I thought.

But before I could reach that extreme, all the confusion slammed to a halt and I whammed against the floor. I kept absolutely still as I waited and wondered. Then a long moaning sigh rushed through the belly. Its wind stirred my feathers. I realized the whale was dead.

In the dark distance, I could see Kapok, her light a faint glow. She carried the lamp in her coils—but away, not towards me.

"Wait!" I yelled. "Come back. I know I made a mistake. But in my defense, I never really touched the lamp. I just drank a little of the oil, that's all. You didn't say anything about the oil."

"It doesn't matter now." Kapok's cool, sober voice echoed to me. "It's over. I must go on."

"No, please. I think I need you. I'm sure I do."

"I knew you'd bring trouble before we even met. Nonetheless, I had to help you. I had to feed you. It was all part of the plan."

"What do you mean? What plan? What plan?"

"I had to feed Raven. I had to save Raven, though I knew Raven would do as Raven has done, no matter what I said."

"I'm just impetuous at times, as we all are," I said. "Anyway, if you're not mad at me, why must you leave? Come back and we'll talk over what happened and next time, I won't be so stupid."

"You are innocent," she answered, her voice fading as the light of her spiral disappeared in the darkness. "Your mistakes are only mistakes if you keep making them."

"Well, I think I've learned a lesson here. We can begin again with another whale. Kapok? Hello? Kapok? Can you still hear me?"

No response. The lamp light was a flickering speck and then nothing. The stomach was again a black cave.

And again, I stumbled about, groping blindly. Unless I found a way out soon, I'd end up a dead bird in a dead whale—these sulfurous fumes would suffocate me.

Finally, in desperation, I stabbed and stabbed at the slick thick stomach wall.

How does one accomplish the impossible? Well, in this instance, I put my fear to positive use. With frantic pecking, gouging, and yanking, I managed to carve a hole through the side of the whale in short time. I then squeezed out into the fresh light of a new day.

The whale had beached itself. Ironically, I now had a nice slab of blubber to feed upon.

Then, as my eyes adjusted to the sun's glare, I found a most welcome sight: ravens, ravens all around me. They stood on the beach; they perched on the rocks or in the nooks and crannies of the nearby sea cliff. The blue whale hide was already pockmarked from their drilling.

"Welcome, brother!" A stocky young raven hopped up to me and spread his wings in greeting. "Will you join us in our feast?"

Part III

Yes, I did feel some guilt over destroying the whale. But I comforted myself with the thought that I'd provided many meals for a raven flock.

In any case, Kapok said this event had been ruled by fate. Could it be another instance of accelerated learning? I hadn't gone into The Land of Tales, yet perhaps I'd slipped into another Raven story. Maybe that happened to some when they needed the learning experience. Considering the course of my life so far, I'd most likely be among that some.

But I hoped not. Those accelerated experiences left me so discombobulated. And not a lot smarter, it seemed. Hadn't I made the same mistake, again and again, just in different settings and with different creatures and things?

Only later did I realize: not so hard, upon reflection, to see a mistake. But much harder to stop myself from making it again, when the opportunity again presents itself.

Anyway, at that point in my life, I didn't want to be Raven, I wanted to be *a raven*, a common raven. I felt I needed a stable life and that's what my new-found flock seemed to offer. It felt right to be among these simple, straight-forward folk. Though the flock had an elder council, its true leaders were Kreck (the one who'd welcomed me) and his wife, Brok. So wise, so patient, though just as young I was. I felt ashamed of myself in their presence.

Kreck's solid disposition matched his short, stocky frame. At first glance, he seemed to lack distinction, but Kreck was smart enough to know his limitations and secure enough not to be threatened by someone of my breadth of experience. He patiently unwound my story from me as we chewed on strips of whale flesh.

I told him how I'd lost my family in the war between the flocks, and of my guilt following that tragedy. Then I described how I'd wandered through the desert aimlessly, hardly conscious of myself.

I felt I needed to tell all of my story, so I decided to violate the secret of those shamans-in-training: I told of The Land of Tales. I believe I made the right choice. Knowledge should not be kept private, but shared— though I'll admit: the consequences of my revelation have not always been positive.

Yes, I told how I'd entered and exited The Land of the Death, how I'd then fallen into the traces of all those stories, and how, afterwards, destiny had led me to the ocean and thrown me into the belly of that whale.

Then, because I'd gone on for so long, I sort of glossed over the part about my oil frenzy.

During the telling I found, to my surprise, that the war between the flocks seemed of a different time. Did I still feel guilty? Yes, but now the feeling didn't seem as dark, as heavy.

Perhaps, just perhaps, by sharing the experience with Kapok, then with Kreck, I was like the prisoner who loosens his chains by expanding his chest. I could breathe more freely now.

Yes, but the reprieve was really only temporary.

By the time I'd finished telling my story, twilight had deepened into night. I was now the center of attention—the whole flock had gathered round to listen. At the end, they remained silent for a long, still moment. Waves broke on the shore, then sizzled back down the sand. Suddenly Kreck lifted his beak. His sharp cry broke the air open; the stars swelled in brightness. It was the purest raven song I'd ever heard. Through it, Kreck acknowledged the gift of my story.

All the flock, every single one of them, then joined with him. Their voices become one with the sounds of an ocean exploding against the rocks. This music lifted something within me, something I'd sensed before but never fully experienced until now and still could not label—except to say: it had strength of meaning felt.

In that moment, I knew I belonged here. I had finally found my home.

Following that grand welcome, the flock took me to their roost—a dense juncture of brush, boulders, marsh, and evergreen trees. I fell asleep to the distant hissings and clashings of the sea.

I had been born and raised in the desert and despite the infernal heat and searing winds, I'd found a fullness of life there. Sometimes, when the clear night chill sparkled the air, I'd felt pure to the core.

But here was a much different land with a much different clime. This great coast had a spirit of life new to me. The air was wet and dense. Tall trees brushed right up against the sun. Water dripped from needles and leaves, filling the forest with a quiet cacophony. Moss softened gray stones. This world had a smoother but deeper texture; it was a place of moisture and prisms, of gentle light. Here, I could nestle into some warm place inside myself, take what I found there, then fold back out.

Kreck's flock was as generous as the land where they lived. This community pretended not to notice my strangeness—that odd aura that hummed about me. I understood that recent experiences had made my natural peculiarity even more peculiar. But I hoped, that by remaining here, I could become a little more ordinary. In time, maybe I'd become just as cheerful and direct as the ravens of this flock. Hopefully, I'd mellow and never again feel that desire for freedom, experienced in my youth. That freedom had resulted in the pain of being lost and confused.

In such a rich world, why would I ever desire something more?

Maybe you're thinking: sooner or later, he will desire something more—something he can't find in this place.

If so, you would be wrong.

Kreck and I quickly became close friends, despite our differences. From him, I gained an understanding of my new locale.

"The mist you feel creeping under your feathers always comes with this season," he told me. "Our winters are cool, but not cold. Summers are mild."

Perched on a bare whale rib, we looked out over a frothy green sea. Sudden gusts exploded approaching waves into plumes of white.

"My brother," I said, "this is the perfect place for me."

"Glad to have you here."

I waited a beat, then added, "Last night, as I settled down to roost, a mysterious sound came to me. Erratic and fluted, it echoed through the trees. A sense of wonder held me fast."

"Oh yeah?"

I described in further detail how the song had held my spirit with its beauty and how, after regaining some measure of composure, I'd located its source: high in a nearby tree, stood a lovely young female silhouetted by the half-moon. I noted the long graceful beak with delicate pin feathers about the nostrils. The tail, with its sharp neat lines, was a dream of perfection.

Extending her full neck, she would pour out her song. But after just a few moments, she would stop abruptly and hop to another branch. Again, she would let the music flow from her heart. But as before, would cut it off short. She followed this pattern through the evening. The way she started and stopped and jumped about the tree maddened me. My brain burned with a purple flame.

No other birds roosted nearby. Obviously, she did not know of my presence. She wanted to release her song, but as privately as possible.

In that music, I heard the restless stir of feelings that can not be named: a longing of the spirit, complex and opaque. But even as these feelings strapped her, choked her, they also gave her breath.

"Yeah, yeah, I know the one you're talking about," Kreck said.

"So, my question is: is she available?'

"Uh huh."

"Wonderful, that's wonderful indeed! You see, I'm sure she's the one for me. I don't know how much time I spent in The Land of Tales, so I can't say for certain how old I am. All I know is: I'm overdue. You know what I mean. I need a mate and I want a mate. But not just anyone. As I said, I'm sure that songstress is the right one for me. Don't ask me how I know because I don't know how I know. I just know. I want to settle down and live a normal raven life with her. That's all I want."

Kreck dipped his head and flexed his toes on the rib.

"What's wrong?" I asked.

"I spoke with the elders last night. They believe you have been sent here to become our shaman."

"But you already have a shaman."

"No one trusts him anymore. Any time anyone comes to him now, he just criticizes. He berates. So, even when he's right, no one listens. But more often than not, they don't even bother with him. Not so useful these days, that crusty toad.

"We're offering you a position of honor, won't you even consider? The flock needs you, needs your help. I believe you came here for a reason. You arrived in such a miraculous way. Seems to me to be the design of destiny."

"Yes, I know I'm an odd one," I said. "Yes, I'm different. But not special, not really. I'm certainly no shaman. I went through some weird times, that's all. Besides, I haven't done the necessary training."

"Certain things can't be taught. A certain predisposition is needed. I believe I see that in you. As well as a strength gained from experience. And the ability to draw from the depths. Perhaps that's most important. The mumbo jumbo of the rituals can be learned easy enough. As for the rest of the training...plenty of shamans never did any training at all. It's not so crucial, I've heard. So, I ask again: will you be our shaman?"

Kreck's plea was torture to me. I felt obligated to this flock because they'd welcomed me in without hesitation. "First, let me talk to that shaman of yours," I said. "Perhaps he's been misunderstood. Don't give up on the old bird yet."

To my regret, the honey-throated female did not show herself that evening. Occasionally, I thought I heard her song echoing from the far distance. But when I stopped to listen, only the dripping of the trees sounded in the emptiness.

The next day, I flew to the shaman's roost, perched

on a branch outside his tree hollow, and cawed three times. After a tedious wait, the old bird finally poked his head out. He didn't seem happy to see me.

What was my plan? My plan had no real plan to it. I would just trust the moment and hope the right words came to me.

As he hopped onto the branch, the shaman lost his balance and fluttered his wings, accidentally hitting me on the snoot. Then, after settling down, he inflated his chest, stuck his beak up, and assumed a worldly attitude. I wanted to laugh at that squat body and those stubby legs. To be honest, he looked more like a crow. Perhaps that was part of his problem with the flock.

"What is it now?" he croaked. "Let me guess—you want to know what to do. Ha! Everybody expects me to do their thinking for them, that's what their problem is. I've told them that what I say comes from the Master Raven. They accept that—when the message is to their liking. If not, they criticize me."

I had to admit, the old geezer made sense. In any case, I wanted to test him with a question of my own.

"Grandfather," I said, "I'll cut straight to the point. My visit here concerns a young female whose song I heard the other evening. I stopped my breath so that I might catch every distant note. Now, I am under a spell that logic and daylight can not dispel. My heart refuses to be denied. And yet, I still wonder: is this union meant to be?"

"Forget it," the shaman cawed. "Won't work out. You need to move on. The sooner the better."

I knew he was wrong. I felt certain this flock was my destiny. I'd move on only if forced. The shaman probably knew the flock wanted me to replace him. Yes, that's why he told this lie.

"I'm sure I've finally found my home," I said

defiantly.

"Forget it. You'll fly alone all the days of your life. Get out now before you do any damage."

Since the old codger refused to listen, I said a simple "thank you" and dropped from his tree.

I hesitated before returning to the roosting place that evening. Unfortunately, Kreck and his friends had waited up for me.

"Oh my, I sure am tired," I lied to them. "I really would like to talk, my brothers, my sisters, but I'd probably fall asleep mid-breath."

"Please, Brother Roe," Kreck said, "give us your opinion of the shaman. You know how we value your insight."

"All I will say for now is: you must leave your shaman alone for the next two days. Then, when you return to him, listen with a different ear. I plan to work with him and help that bird sort things out."

The ravens all hung their heads and shuffled their feet. They knew, just as I did, that their shaman was a lost cause. I'd disappointed them. Nonetheless, I still had no intention of offering myself up as the new shaman.

But how could I possibly solve this problem in just two days? I wished I'd given myself more time. I had to work fast.

That evening I flew to the highest limb of the tallest redwood in the forest and buckled myself down. A strong wind slapped my wings. The limb swung to and fro. But I just sank my claws deeper into the bark and fixed my mind on one thing: tonight I must visit The Realm of the One-In-All, the spiritual home of all ravens, the place where all the knowledge of Raven is kept. I must petition the Master Raven.

My wish was soon answered. I felt myself lift from my physical body after only a few moments. I then ascended through dark dense gray that gradually brightened into white—the soft white of clouds. I came to rest in a spacious dome with many branching tunnels: the center of The Realm. Hak then appeared before me.

I knew this old attendant from previous trips. Hak exuded a noble simplicity that I found reassuring. In time, he would show how I need not go into The Land of the Tales in order to learn what that place had to teach. I could see the stories and learn their messages by looking down from above, down from The Realm into The Land. Then afterward, I could share the wisdom of those tales with the flock.

That's not to say I didn't slip into a tale and live its story from time to time. Often it happened in a dream —the way most live these stories, I believe.

To be honest, I've lived a tale even after seeing its message from above. I had to learn some of those lessons again and again before the message finally stuck —before I was finally able to become aware of a mistake while I was making the mistake and could stop myself.

At this point in my life, I wasn't so familiar with The Realm. Past forays had involved just short conversations with Hak as we flew through some of the many loops and warps of the place. Despite the brevity of these visits, I'd felt wiser—stronger—when I returned. A feeling so easily lost—lost as soon as I encountered conflict in the lower world again. In such conflict, my lower instinct would usually triumph over my higher instinct. I was young then. But the war within, in my experience, never really ends.

I told Hak of my purpose. He did not blink; he did

not argue. I'd expected more resistance—a word of caution, perhaps. Ravens usually petition the Master Raven through the flock shaman. And then only for major decisions, major dilemmas. But even in those cases, an answer is not guaranteed. What's the determining factor? The information you seek must be judged to be for the benefit of all. Perhaps, in that regard, my intent was not so pure. Nonetheless, I felt I must try—though rejection was quite serious. After three refusals, you can never petition again during your lifetime. Afraid to waste their three chances, many often wait too long—some never petition even once.

"Before, when you came here, we flew together," Hak said. "But this time we must walk. Follow me."

The old attendant turned and began to shuffle down a long tunnel made of sturdy white cloud. I trailed after him. A single feather stood up from the disheveled mess on his crown. Hak had a slow nodding step. Ever so often, he'd jerk his head as if he had a crick in his neck.

I could barely feel my feet touch down. Wisps of white cloud purled around my ankles.

The white light of the tunnel soon faded to gray twilight, then deepened to total darkness. I could no longer see Hak, so I followed the sound of his rasping breath.

"Stop." he said. "Wait here."

"How long before I know if I'm accepted?"

"Watch your impatience—your fear. Clear your mind as best you can. Focus on your problem—in your heart, not your head. Thought obstructs, but feeling clears. Sincerity is key when petitioning the Master Raven."

"Well, I feel very sincere right now," I told him.

"When you are done here, I will return."

After Hak had gone, I took a deep breath, flexed my

talons, and tried to focus my heart on this one question: "How can I replace the shaman with someone who will serve them well?"

But oh—the desire behind that question awakened the hope of a dream and the fear of a major disappointment. What if the Master Raven said I was not to marry the honey-throated female? What if the message was: "you are the one"? The thought of such a life!—to live alone in a tree hollow or some cave and be besieged by the needs of others all day and into the night.

If only I could have that young songtress for my own. Our life together would be the perfect circle. But no—I'd surely be told she couldn't be mine. I should forget my petition and leave The Realm pronto.

But before I could take a step, a great yowling wind hit me, lifting me off my feet and spinning me up and away through the darkness. Plumes of cloud swirled about me.

A moment later, the wind set me back down. The plumes settled into cloud and the cloud gradually lightened until I could see the Master Raven suspended before me—just far enough not to be too close. Its right talon was bunched into a fist; its left talon, spread out like a fan. The wings were stretched away from the body—feathered draperies with the deep soft darkness of soot. The head was in profile, displaying to full effect the sharp black beak and a dark eye as hard and as smooth and as shiny as the legendary black pearl.

The luminous tufts of cloud only accentuated the weighty opaqueness of the Master Raven. Before me was our wellspring—our source: the form and essence of all ravens. A concept that continues to evolve as we evolve.

By now, I'd gone far beyond mere nervousness—I stood petrified, weak with this realization: I had no choice now but to surrender the dreamy desires of my puny self. No choice—I'd be forced to serve a greater good, though unworthy of the task, a task beyond my capabilities. No choice—I was not the one in control.

The massive head turned until its dark eyes stared down that long black beak to focus on little me. The power emanating from the Master Raven became even more intense now—came to me in waves, waves with crests and troughs like an ocean breathing. This force permeated my being, eradicating all fear as my spirit rose to accept what it could not reject. In the void of the moment, from a center of absolute calm, a message came to me, a communication without sound, a knowing: "Tomorrow when you awaken, you must leave your roost immediately and fly due north. Fly until you come to a spring that cuts between two boulders. On one side of the spring, you will find an oak. On the other, a tall pine tree. Wait atop the boulder under the pine. You will receive your answer there."

In the next moment, the clouds began to swirl again and I lost the Master Raven. A blast of wind tossed me up, threw me around for a long short while, then set me gently down. Again, I found myself in total darkness, total silence. I felt the relief of release, yet the break was still a pain.

Once again, I heard Hak's rasping breath. The old attendant pecked me on the shoulder. I followed him back through the tunnel. The darkness faded into twilight; the twilight brightened into light.

"You feel both relieved and uneasy," Hak said.

"I get the feeling the bad news has only been temporarily delayed."

"Just because you fear something doesn't mean it will happen."

Without another word, the old attendant shuffled off down the soft hallway, his tail feathers brushing fluffs of cloud. I wanted to say something, but couldn't think to speak. A moment later, I began to descend to the earth realm.

The next morning, I woke before sunrise, shook my feathers out, then slipped down through the trees, heading due north.

I flew all morning without a break, searching for the spring that cut between two boulders. As the sun neared its zenith, I began to wonder if I had missed the spot. What if I never found that spring? I could be in traveler's limbo 'til the end of my days.

Then suddenly I sighted water gushing whitely between two gray boulders. A broad oak shadowed one rock. A tall pine stood above the other.

I dove down, settled myself on the boulder under the pine, and began my wait.

This place seemed most ordinary. My sensors detected no unusual vibes.

As the sun began to creep its way back down the sky, my legs grew stiff. I shuffled my wings, trying to relieve my restlessness.

Then quite suddenly, black clouds came in over the trees. The air sizzled with the anticipation of rain.

"Oh great," I thought. "Not only am I stuck here for no telling how long, but now I'm going to get rained on as well."

But I did not dare seek cover. The Master Raven had told me to wait atop the rock. Whatever discomfort I experienced now would be nothing compared to the pain brought on by going against guidance.

The air flashed white—an eerie light. Then a rumble of thunder rolled from one end of the sky to the other. I hunkered down, feeling that a lightning bolt could cleave me at any moment.

The wind suddenly rushed through the trees and kept rushing. Blown leaves slapped onto my back. I clawed the boulder and tried to hang on. My stomach felt so weak.

Then abruptly, all became still. But I knew this quiet was only a brief reprieve. And yes—in the next moment, a thick raindrop splattered the top of my head. I huddled my wings together as the rain began in earnest. It bounced off my back like a fall of pebbles. Again, the gale raged through the forest, making all a green blur. I dug my toes in deeper, but couldn't get a solid grip on that rain-slick rock.

The wind began to sneak under me. I lowered my center of gravity, but could not stop the wind from gradually lifting me from my perch. I hovered in the air for a long, agonizing moment, my wings beating helplessly against the tempest. Then abruptly, a gust slammed me sideways. I narrowly dodged one tree, then another. I tried steering myself down to the base of the boulder, but could not fight through the stiff bluster. I feared that at any moment I would whop into a tree and burst asunder.

Then, through the cacophony of wind and rain, I heard a voice—faraway it was, yet distinct. The voice said, "Yes...yes...yes."

A moment later, the voice spoke again, this time saying, "No...no...no."

I knew it was the voice of a spirit—the sorrow of a spirit sometimes brings on a storm.

"Yes...yes...yes," the spirit repeated with notes of melancholia. "No...no...no."

As I continued to flap and flutter amid the trees, I yelled, "What do you mean to say, spirit? I don't understand."

"Yes...yes...yes," it said sadly. "No...no...no."

"What do you want, please! Don't equivocate."

"Yes...yes...yes." The voice seemed closer now. "No...no...no."

My wing joints ached at the shoulder. My throat was raw from rain. "What's wrong with you, dammit! Speak sense!"

The force of the storm eased a bit. "I am lost...lost...lost," the spirit moaned.

"Well, stop this rain, stop this wind, and I'll try to help you. I know a lot about being lost and confused. Set me down!"

Abruptly, the squall stopped. Caught off guard, I plunked straight down and bounced on roots and rocks before jagging my claws into the earth.

As I staggered to my feet, the black clouds began to break apart. Sunlight suddenly splintered through the trees. "Thank you, spirit." I forced a smile.

A golden sun shone inside a water drop sliding down a leaf. Near me, a transparent-gray shadow, nebulous and wiggly, hovered over a flat stone.

"Tell me, spirit, why are you so lost?"

"I can not find a body to live in," the shadow whined in a thin voice, a voice neither male nor female.

"But you are a spirit. You can inhabit the form of any creature, any creature you wish."

The spirit then explained that it had experimented with one form after another. As a bear, it had enjoyed the strength of its limbs, but didn't like feeling sluggish all winter. As a salmon, it'd loved life in the water. But hated fighting its way upstream to spawn. Its high flights as an eagle were exhilarating, yes. But the solitary life had left the spirit feeling forlorn. Each time the spirit had tried a new form, it'd discovered a problem.

"Well, I have the perfect solution," I announced.

"Why not try life as a raven? We also fly quite high, you know. Yet we're social—you need never feel alone. No seasonal problems—you won't have to hibernate or migrant. No predators to harry you. Plus, you'll be handsome, intelligent—the best of all birds.

"In fact, I have a nice flock already picked out for you. They live by the sea. A lovely place. And get this: you'll be their shaman. A position of great respect. You'll be exalted by all."

"I don't know...I don't know," the spirit mused.

"Well, give it a try, at least. See if it works for you. If it doesn't, you can always do a swift exit."

I continued in this manner for some time. Finally, after much waffling, the spirit half-heartedly agreed to my plan.

To be honest, considering the nature of this spirit, I felt half-hearted about the plan too. But hadn't the Master Raven directed me here? In any case, I needed a substitute.

Late that night, after returning to the flock, I settled down on a branch outside the shaman's tree hollow and listened. The old mite-mat wheezed in his sleep.

With great focus of will, I reached in with my talons and grabbed him by the neck. His beak sprang open in reflex. Being deep in a dream, he didn't wake, though his body spasmed.

"Okay, spirit, climb in. Come on, hurry up."

"Yes yes yes no no no," the spirit said. "What if there isn't room enough?"

"You know he has to leave once you hop in. Now get on with it."

"Not sure not sure."

That geezer shaman began to shake his wings. If he woke fully, the spirit wouldn't be able to enter. But though I begged, that damn shadow kept balking. Finally, I lost patience—I snagged the shade with my free talon, shoved it down the old bird's throat, then held the beak shut.

A flurry of flapping, gagging, and feathers followed. The legs shot out. The eyes bulged open. The entire body went into a paroxysm of thrashing and kicking. Fearing I might kill the host, I threw the bird back down.

The body shuddered and jerked for a few moments, then settled. I waited in suspense.

The spirit blinked his raven eyes as if stunned.

"You okay?" I asked.

"Yes yes yes," he said. "No no no."

"Excellent," I said.

A green translucent shape rose through the dark branches like a wobbly bubble.

"I suppose you're mad at me," I yelled to the spirit of the former shaman.

"Not at all," the spirit called back. "I was ready to leave. The moment I saw you, I knew you'd deliver me. I knew you were the one. Thank you."

"Glad to help."

"Just remember what I said. What you think you want is not to be. You won't be allowed to stay where you are."

I started to protest, but in the next moment, the green light of the spirit began to flicker. Then the bubble broke into green dust, soon lost in the darkness of night.

The next morning, I told the flock that the shaman had seen the error of his abusive ways. He felt frustrated at times, that's all—he wanted them to use their own wisdom when dealing with the small dilemmas of life. Being overly reliant on him would only weaken them. Yes, they should seek his guidance, but only when circumstances warranted.

Ah, but old habits are hard to break. A young raven soon set herself down outside the tree hollow and asked if she would find a mate that season

"Yes yes yes," the new shaman said. "No no no."

"You're right," she said with embarrassment. "I must learn to use my own intuition."

Then a young male, eager to hunt, visited the shaman. "Will I find fresh carrion if I go north?"

"Yes yes yes," the shaman replied. "No no no."

"You're right," this raven said with embarrassment. "I must learn to use my own intuition."

Then one of the elders came to test the shaman, to see if he'd improved. "What kind of winter can we expect?" he asked. "Cold or unseasonably warm? The usual rain or a few more days of sun?"

"Yes yes yes," said the shaman. "No no no."

"He takes great care in how he answers now," the elder reported to his colleagues. "He's grown wiser in just two days time."

The flock believed the change in the shaman was due to my wise instruction. They were even more impressed with me now.

And so, when the family of the honey-throated female heard of my intention, they took me by the wing and led me to her. They were quite eager to have their daughter marry someone of such distinction.

After I introduced myself, she batted her lids dumbly as if she didn't understand the meaning of my visit. I began to wonder if she was one of those whose mind did not mirror the beauty and intelligence of her deep spirit.

Hoping for the best, I plunged ahead. "I heard you sing the other night," I said. "I've wanted to approach you before now. But felt awkward."

"Why? You wanted to prove yourself first?" she asked. She sounded intelligent. And sarcastic.

While I fumbled, searching for the appropriate response, she continued, "So how did you get the shaman to change his ways?"

"I'd like to tell you, but I can't. I'm sorry. You see, my instructions came from the Master Raven."

"You petitioned the Master Raven?"

"Well, yes, I did." I rattled a leaf with my foot.

"Go ahead and brag—you've earned it."

My head felt dizzy. She'd begun by acting dumb, then had cut me down, then had finished me off with a compliment. I immediately realized two things: first, that we would be together, and second, that I was getting more than I'd bargained for.

"So how do you make those beautiful sounds?" I asked her.

"I honestly don't know. Something comes upon me at night—something within forces its way up and out. If I tried to stop it, I'd pass out. I have no choice, really, and the song flows naturally, so why should I take credit?"

"Is that why you choose to keep it private?"

"No. I am proud. But also shy."

"I'm surprised you haven't picked a mate yet," I said. You must've had plenty of offers."

"The eligible all know about my singing, that it can strike any time of night. You are a great relief to my father and mother."

Allo was her name. Drawn first by that beautiful voice, I now began to love her for her eccentricity.

After a brief but weighty courtship, Allo and I announced the match. The ceremony took place in a clearing shadowed by massive redwoods. First, the whole flock made a circle around Allo and me. Then the new/old shaman stepped forward to sanctify our union.

He shook his wings out with much pomp, then looked around at the flock with an air of authority.

"Yes yes yes... no no no," he began. "Today we celebrate the sacredness of this conjunction. Two become one, one become two. Yes yes yes, no no no. What I mean to say I mean...what I what..."

My hope had been: the yes-no spirit would respond to the requirements of his new job by drawing from the same deep pool used by all shamans. If not now, then later. But no—I could see his channel would never be clear enough for the information to flow through—at least, not in any coherent way. Even so, I knew he might last in this position—just like other clogged channels I've met.

"A division of two spirits united," he continued. "We give this day...knowing they'll bring it back. And so it will be...and so it was. Yes yes yes, no no no."

Pleased with his oration, the shaman then shouted out a loud caw.

I hung my head and scraped the ground with my talon. What an embarrassment, this fake!

But to my surprise, all the congregation flapped their wings in appreciation of the speech. They were still quite taken with the fool. He could do no wrong.

In response, the shaman stepped back and spread his wings with a dramatic flourish. Yes, I'd provided the flock with a real nincompoop. In time, they'd see my so-called miracle for the failure it was. And then they might very well ring my neck.

Hoping to cut this ridiculous ceremony short, I stretched to my full height and addressed the group, thanking them for this special day, and for accepting me into their flock. Then, in case they ever did think of ringing my neck, I reminded them that I was just an ordinary bird, quite capable of making mistakes like anyone else.

Then I ended by saying Allo and I would return in the fall with a brood that would make the flock shine even brighter than before.

As the assembly raised their voices in loving raven song, my mate and I took wing. We would weave our way through the forest until we found the perfect roosting place.

Nothing describes the harmony of true union like mated ravens in flight—the way they flow together, each mirroring the other for long stretches, then one taking the lead and then the other. Allo and I dipped and soared and wheeled and spun together, often with only a breath of space separating the tips of our wings— a sparking charge popped whenever we touched those feather tips together.

Three days of flying led us to a nook in a craggy rock cliff deep within a forest. Intuitively we knew: here would be our roost. A waterfall leapt and leapt down the face of that cliff—sometimes we'd feel the mist on a sudden gust. We thought we heard a low rapturous moan behind the churn of that fall. But maybe the sound came from our romantic imagination. More likely, a spirit ceaselessly weeping in joy sang the history of this Earth.

A raven's nest is a paradox of life: durable yet so soft; made of ordinary things, yet a marvel in its totality. Thick twigs form the outer rim, while a weave of leaves, pine needles and down creates the tender inner circle.

Often the male raven merely watches as the female constructs this haven. Knowing he must provide for her during the period of incubation, the male takes this time to do as he pleases. He does fancy figures and somersaults in the air while she works.

But I want you to know: most of my male friends reject that way. And so do I. Allo and I built our nest together—and with only an occasional disagreement. I don't like to brag, but I must say, through the harmony of our labor, we built an exquisite matrix.

Yes, I'd traveled far from the fledgling I'd once been. Far from the young bird that wanted only freedom and adventure. When I'd realized the freedom I'd imagined, I'd not found the joy I'd imagined. As for adventure...this new life with Allo was another adventure into the unknown. Not as strange as my previous wild flights, no, but incredible, nonetheless. Consider this fascinating turn: for the first time in my life, I felt in synch with the world around me. In synch with that sensibly-woven paradoxical nest...in synch with that moaning waterfall...in-synch with the green caterpillar creeping over that moss on the rock...in-synch with the moonlight that draped our nighttime world with silver and shadow.

And in synch with Allo—although after our first few nights together, her singing did begin to rankle me. Just a little bit. She might erupt into song in the middle of the night, bursting the warm bubble of my sleep. But no circle is perfect. Only ideas are perfect. In any case, the sense of peace and security I'd found in this new life seemed solid.

Oh, but I should have known better. Hadn't life already taught me that security did not truly exist?

I suppose I wanted to ignore what I knew. Can you blame me? The life I was now living was far better than any life I'd lived before.

Eight days after we'd completed the nest, the time

came—the time that brings a crescendo to the anxiety of hopeful parents. The whole forest seemed to hold its breath for a long, tense moment. Then, after a deep sigh, that wonderful green world began to breath again. Allo sagged with relief, spent from her labors. For the rest of that evening, she just stared into the darkness, resting in the tranquility of new motherhood. For once, she did not break into song. Four strong, green eggs held the secret of the brood to come.

I think now is a good time to tell the truth about Noah and the ark...

Too often people forget that after forty days and forty nights of rain, Noah first sent forth a raven, not a dove, from his big boat. When the raven did not return, Noah then shoved the dove out into the new world.

Unlike the darker avian, this good little bird came back with a green sprig in its beak. And so, ever since, people see the dove as pure in intent—aspirational—and see ravens as self-serving—dark-hearted. In fact, some believe that after that incident, God cursed the raven and made it to dine only on corpses.

Well, I'm here to assure you, that's no curse. Anyone who believes that nonsense has never tasted the sweet salty blood of a fresh carcass.

Anyway, you're probably wondering what happened to the raven after it left the ark.

Well, before Noah's family and all the animals set out upon the waters, God decreed that no creature of that menagerie should breed while aboard. But according to rumor, the two ravens disobeyed that order. As the storm raged and the waters dashed the ark about, the ravens found comfort by engaging in the sacred act that brings forth life. At a time of merciless destruction, the ravens said, "Creatures come and creatures go, but life continues unabated!" They were not fornicating, but rejecting death by uniting in love. On that ark, the ravens danced the dance that keeps the circle of life turning.

But for that, captain Noah threatened them with the punishment of death. So as soon as the window opened, those two bid forever farewell to him and his damn ship and took flight.

Lacking any other means of retribution, Noah spread cruel rumors about us ravens for years afterward.

A few days after the first big day came the second big day. All morning, I felt a subtle quiet tension slowly building. Allo sat in the nest as usual, but a bit stiffly. I'd never seen her so agitated. She wouldn't stop preening her feathers. As for myself...I kept jumping to the limb above, then back down again. I remember watching a water drop dangle from the tip of a leaf. I felt like kicking that drop free, but restrained myself.

Only after a long tedious wait did the drop fall—it fell down and down and finally made a tiny plunk in the pool at the bottom of the waterfall.

Suddenly, Allo sat up and straightened her long neck. The pin feathers prickled around her beak. Those black eyes went wide and blank. Slowly, delicately, she lifted herself and stepped to the side of the nest. On one of the green eggs, a tiny hole appeared.

Time seemed to jump several notches at once. In mere moment—or so it seemed—a spindly gray raven-chick rose from the crusts of a shell. Its body swayed on unsure legs. The bulging eyes blinked.

Then in a flicker of sunlight and shade, three more little ravens appeared. Four beaks now opened on extended necks to emit hunger shrieks. Life was already acting on those baby birds, stinging them with air and light and pushing them with basic desire. They cried and they sang.

Ravens name their young immediately after they hatch and without forethought. A name is, of course, a sound. We believe that sound can and should express a truth about the bird so named. But how can you know the truth at first sight? Well, you let the name come to you spontaneously—from your deep knowing: what you intuitively sense about the hatchling's potential. What the newborn bird can be—not what we wish it to become.

Following that belief, we chose Pruk and Ga for the girls and Tok and Kra for the boys. I think the names speak for themselves.

Kra was built of odd pieces: he had thin, magpie legs and one wing hung down a bit. But clumsy though he was, he surged ahead of the others, driven by an eager energy that pushed him out into the world.

Tok was outer-directed as well, but more cautious. Build wide, he had stubby wings and a blunt beak. In thought and action, he moved at a deliberate pace. Because he and I were of such opposite natures, I thought I might have something to give him.

Ga had Tok's physical strength as well as his reserve. She wanted life to come to her, so she could examine it carefully before making a commitment. I knew her aloofness would attract many suitors—and frustrate most. Hopefully, she would learn that humility is a part of grace.

The runt of the batch was Pruk. A bit sickly, but still feisty. She'd often extend that scrawny neck as if trying to get a better look at a world that both confused and amazed her. A relentless curiosity in that sprout— she would linger over any little thing. Isn't that love of life? In a twinkling, she won that special place in the heart reserved for the favorite—I couldn't help it.

However, her keen mind seemed to aim her attention everywhere except toward me. I had to appreciate her from a distance.

Like any brood, I suppose: a mix of flaws and terrific potential, with the flaws being part of that potential. In any case, Allo and I felt quite pleased.

Within days of their hatching, the fledglings dropped from the nest and folded their wings out for the first time. Though they wobbled a bit at the beginning, they soon found a smooth balance in their flight.

Come fall, we would bring them to the flock's roosting place. There, they would learn more about this raven life—including what was expected of them. They would spend a little time with the shaman and be told about The Realm of the One-In-All. Then when spring came, Allo and I would leave them and return to this nook by the waterfall to bring forth another brood.

Following that pattern, our lives would proceed with order and harmony, season after season. Or so I assumed.

But then one evening near the end of summer, this plan collapsed. That night, I woke in the nest with Allo and the brood asleep all around me. For a few moments, I just drowsed, warmed by feelings of love and gratitude. Then the hum of a new sensation began spread through my body. I realized I was being summoned, and the thought filled me with dread—I did not want to go to the Realm of the One-in-All. But a moment later, I felt myself lift from the frame.

I rose quickly in spirit form through the night sky, feeling both wistful and weak. Ravens are rarely summoned and when they are, it's not for the sake of a jolly good time. Usually there's a demand that can not ignored. You're told what you must do and what you must do is probably not something you want to do.

I feared I might lose in my wonderful new life. At the same time, I knew could not argue.

Moonlight shone purple on the dark clouds above me. Then suddenly I was in those clouds—the purple wisps spiraled all around me. The beauty nearly calmed me. But then I found myself in that familiar dense gray fog. Soon—too soon—I stood at the center of The Realm. From all sides of this hub ran long corridors of sturdy white cloud. Going where? Answer that question for yourself.

I found Hak waiting for me, a single feather sticking up from the matted mess atop his crown. He nodded once, but did not speak. Turning, he began to waddle his way down a corridor.

I realized, to my chagrin, that my communication would not be with him. No, I was to return to one I both dreaded and desired.

As I followed Hak, the white light faded to twilight gray, then that grayness gradually deepened into darkness. Hak's upright feather sparkled at its very tip. That bit of light helped lead me through the dense dark. I felt so nervous I could barely step.

Suddenly, the silver spark vanished. In the next instant, a great yowling wind lifted me off my feet, spinning me upwards and away. As before, plumes of cloud snaked around me. As before, I felt weak in the stomach and braced myself against this gale—no use fighting it; flapping was futile.

What a relief when that little tornado set me back down moments later.

As the plumes settled into sturdy cloud and began to lighten, I again found myself standing before the Master Raven. Its head was held in profile, displaying to full effect the sharp black beak and a glossy black-pearl eye. The wings were spread out from the body, dense-black against a white cloud background.

By now, I'd gone beyond extreme anxiety to experience the calm that sometimes comes when we feel utterly helpless.

As before, I felt waves of energy pulsing to me from the Master Raven, then pulsing inside me. These waves flowed from its deep center, a center rich and secret: the very wellspring of life. Our truth.

Yet as I connected with the source, I felt my survival to be in jeopardy. I feared that if I joined with that force, the "I" that was my identity would be lost forever.

The massive head rotated slowly toward me. The dense, dark eyes—eyes that held both everything and nothing—stared down that long black beak at my puny self.

"You must leave this flock you have found." A communique painful in its clarity.

"Where shall we go?" I asked weakly.

"Not 'we'. You must go alone."

I collapsed within. I nearly lost consciousness; my mind swirled with misery. Using what remained of my strength, I tried to slow my vertigo. First, I'd get the details, then I'd pass out.

"Tomorrow morning, fly due east and keep flying until you come to the place you need to be. You'll know that place when you see it."

"And what am I supposed to do there?"

"Wait. Wait and you will learn what must be done."

"Will I be allowed to return afterward?"

"After you do what must be done, you will learn what you must do next."

I desperately wanted to know more, but in the very next instant, I was pulled backward, then caught and tossed again by an upward spiraling wind as clouds swirled about me.

Then, as before, the wind set me back down in the dark. A speck of light glinted from the tip of the feather sticking up from Hak's pate.

Before I could speak, my guide said, "You could answer the question for yourself, if you weren't so afraid of what the answer might be. In any case, I can't tell you."

I knew he was right. And so, I didn't say another word, but followed the old attendant back down the corridor.

I woke my family when I returned to the nest. Allo accepted the news with a dignified sadness and tried to encourage me with hope. I realize nothing I could say would help the fledglings understand. They knew little about The Realm or higher responsibilities. I could not even comfort them with the promise that I'd return. I could only huddle them together under my wings so that we might share our love and our sadness until morning came. Whatever happened, I hope they would keep this memory of me.

By dawn, the others had fallen asleep. So I dropped quietly out of the nest and headed east, moving my wings by rote, without the joy of flight.

The landscape soon began to change. Broad leafy trees replaced the tall redwoods. Then these trees gradually thinned out as the soil became a light powdery brown. Scraggly pines and ragged grass fought for life between slabs of rock.

In the distance, gray mountains jutted straight up from the rolling land.

After I lifted above those peaks, the air felt peppery and coarse in my lungs. I became giddy—oxygen molecules seemed to bubble in my brain. In this drunken state, I forgot some of my pain and actually began to enjoy the scenery and the updrafts of air that gave me an occasional push.

After shooting through a mountain pass, I saw before me a short cliff that overlooked a grassy plain and a lake. Somehow I knew I'd found the place. I landed near the edge of the cliff and began my wait.

I waited with strained patience through three days and three nights, only sleeping when my groggy head absolutely demanded rest. Except for an occasional breeze hushing through the valley, all was still. I thought about Allo and the brood until the pain of loss seemed to numb—to my relief. Yes, I knew that the pain still lived within. But for the time being, I needed to focus on the outer world—to remain alert and ready, in case my reason for being here suddenly revealed itself.

Finally, mid-afternoon on the fourth day, my answer came. In the far distance, a dust cloud moved over a dirt road that cut through the valley. Using my keen raven vision, I spied the cause of that cloud: a wagon that reflected the sun. In short time, that big box came to rest at the edge of the lake, doors popped open, and four humans stepped out. They all stretched their arms wide and took deep breaths as if lacking for air. When they'd recovered a bit, the four then squinted into the bright sunlight and surveyed the peaceful surroundings.

From the outset, I could see that all was not well with these people: they struggled with their equipment, grappling with poles and bags and cases as if angry at the weights and sizes of the physical world.

I knew I was to interact with them in some way, but how or why I could not guess. So I continued to wait near the cliff's edge.

That night, I blinked my eyes awake to find the form of Hak, outlined in blue light, standing beside me. What a privilege!—I knew Hak rarely visited the earth realm.

"So happy to see you, Grandfather," I said, then started right in: "The humans who arrived here today, what am I to do with them?"

Hak stretched his neck to the side as he struggled to adjust to the coarser vibrations of this realm. "You must help them find Raven. That's your job, that's what it is."

"I don't understand."

He shuffled his wings. "Those four humans are trapped. You can tell just by watching them. Something is wrong inside and each knows something's wrong. They've all tried various types of medicine and all feel frustrated because the magical cure remains elusive.

"You must guide them down to Raven—down, all the down to the wise Raven within. Then lead them out and up and then bring them back. Afterwards, they'll be able to access that wisdom for themselves."

"I'm totally confused. I don't know how to guide anyone down and in, then out and up, much less bring them back."

"You do know, you just don't know that you know. Don't worry—you will realize what you know when the time comes.

"But first, you must connect with the humans. Must connect with each one separately for just a few moments—when that person is most open, spiritually speaking. During the connection, you will relay the instructions for the dance you're to do—'The Raven Dance Song', my name for that information. Give the song just as I give it to you now."

"Okay, sure, whatever. Then after I do this thing, can I return to my family?"

"That I cannot say."

"But what are my chances? You must know something."

"I'm not accustomed to this harsh atmosphere. Irritates, agitates. I must get back. Open yourself and I'll give you the instruction song."

I took a deep breath, then Hak leaned over and began to whisper in my ear. His words were a river, a murmuring river—the incantation held me fast.

When he'd finished a few moments later, I could not think to speak—still lost in rapture, I was. But Hak did not wait. His form soon grew mist-like and faded into the night.

Hak had told me everything except what I most needed at the moment: how to proceed, how to connect. Distracted by my wish to return, I'd forgotten to ask about specifics. So when would these humans be most open?

I decided on this first step: I would attract the attention of the four. I thought, once they saw me, they'd want to connect. They'd be open to me.

So, the next morning, I stepped out from the sagebrush and presented myself at the edge of the cliff, in full view of the campers.

While the other three occupied themselves with mundane matters, one scanned the sky and rotated a full circle, surveying the terrain. But somehow he missed me. Finally, I fanned my wings, then turned and waggled my tail feathers to attract his attention.

Only then did the man give a shout and raise his arm to point me out to the others.

For the rest of the day, I strutted around the ledge, moving this way and that, occasionally stopping to caw loud and sharp, then spreading out my wings majestically, then closing those feathered curtains in, over my lowered head, to heighten the mystery. Yes, I put on quite a show. And oh, how those humans lapped it up—they studied my every move. With their awestruck eyes, they seemed to worship me. I couldn't help but feel I was something special.

But then the tedium of the act set in. I felt relieved when the four retired to their camp, late afternoon.

In my fanciful imagination, I believed my plan had worked. I'd stirred the fascination of those campers— their sense of mystery. They be more open now, more open to my message, the instructions Hak had given. But I would not confront anyone directly. No, I'd wait until all four had put the noise of their conscious minds to rest—these humans obviously had a lot of noise. Way too much.

With that in mind, I swooped down from the cliff and came to rest at the edge of their campsite, keeping myself well-hidden in the dark while watching them as they prepared for their evening meal.

A man whose chest had sunk to the level of his stomach poked the campfire with a stick. This fellow had a slow waddling walk that told of deep fatigue—the simplest task seemed a challenge for him. Shadows deepened his furrowed brow.

I could feel the tension between him and a woman that I took to be his mate. As he knelt at the fire, she stood over him with her feet planted apart in a challenging stance. Her body was so rigid I could hear her vertebrae crackle when she shifted her weight.

"Shouldn't it should be done by now, Roy?" she

asked.

"Almost, Kay, almost.   Taking longer than I expected, dear."

The woman named Kay stared down at man's bowed head as if trying, with her intense stare, to add to the load he already carried.

"Maybe he's using Kay to help him develop his fortitude," I thought to myself.   "No wonder her musculature seems so taut—it's quite a task he's asked of her. Day after day, she toils in this manner, chained by agreement to this fellow Roy. But I suppose, by performing this difficult job, she strengthens her own fortitude as well. I see what's at work here: they can't stand each other, yet they need each other, but they need each other because they can't stand each other.

"A pact made between their secret selves. No, I don't think they're actually aware of this agreement. If they knew, they'd probably stop doing what they're doing."

"Stew's ready, I guess," Roy said, standing up all of a sudden as if unable to bear the tension any longer. "Hot enough to scald the hair off a pig. So be careful." He forced a laugh.

A lanky younger man sat on a rock nearby. He had a long serious face and yellow hair that splashed against his cheeks. A woman sat at his feet. She hunkered inward, a posture similar to that of the praying mantis. Her cheekbones bulged against translucent skin. Deep sockets shadowed blue eyes. I soon discovered her name was Gloria. The man was Keith.

With my keen raven perception, I could see Gloria wanted someone to rescue her and so, she was always trying to rescue others.   Keith liked the fawning attention—he secretly felt insecure. But because he hated feeling so weak, he felt compelled to ignore his mate.

I realized the plan at work here: after repeated rejection, Gloria would finally realize she needed to heal herself. Then after they broke, Keith would suffer the anger of pain and confusion. But as he struggled through that mess, he'd learn the truth of his wound and then began to doctor himself.

What wonderful arrangements! If only these four could see what I saw so clearly—what they were doing to themselves and each other so that they might change. But who was I to criticize their blindness? Many times, many times, I'd fooled myself so that I might change in the ways I needed to change.

The four humans carried their plates and bowls over to a blanket spread on the bare desert earth. Insects batted about the light of a lamp.

The quiet was weighted with tension.

Finally, Keith spoke. "Roy, tomorrow I'd like to shoot some footage of the two of you inspecting the area, doing your usual ornithological fieldwork. I want to show you and Kay operating as a team."

Roy lowered his head and hesitated for a moment. "Don't you think we should focus on the bird?" he said. "You don't know how lucky we were this afternoon. This raven subspecies tends to shy away from humans. Two years ago, we spotted a pair near here, but haven't seen them since. Hopefully, the one we saw today will show up again tomorrow—we need to be on the lookout. So maybe don't concentrate on us. You can get that footage later, right? Look, I know you know your work better than I do. I'm not trying to telling you what to...what I'm concern about...Well, I guess it should be your decision. What the heck. Shoot whatever you want tomorrow. We'll do whatever you say. Right, Kay?"

The silence emanating from Kay now dominated the little circle. You could hear the breeze whisking down from the hills and across the lake. Roy knew not to press.

After dinner, Roy, Kay, and Gloria stared into the campfire as Keith rattled on about his plans for the project. Eventually, Kay heaved a big sigh, stood up, and stalked off to her tent. Keith finally seemed to run out of words around this time. The three campers then rose and prepared for bed.

The fire spit and hissed as if voicing the campers' unspoken anger. I waited until the lamplight had died behind the skin of both tents. Then, to the sound of water lapping the shore, I crept my way to Keith and Gloria's abode.

As Keith wrestled with his sleeping bag, Gloria sat and stared at him with the frightened intensity of a boxed-in animal.

"I don't know how much more of this I can stand!" she whispered.

"What? What the hell are you talking about?"

"You know what—those two. If they'd only let up once in awhile. Pick pick pick, that's all they ever do. And without hardly saying a word. Such hostility!—it's in every little thing they do, in the very air. It gets so damn tense I can barely breathe. At first, I thought it was all her. Then I realized he's just as bad—acting like such a victim. You want to make a documentary on them?—then let it be about the evils of passive-aggressive behavior! Call it 'The Dynamite Duo'! Babe, I'm damn near done in."

Keith's glare shone like cat eyes in the darkness.

"Would you please, please stop overinflating things!" he shouted in a whisper. "I mean, who are you to criticize them? Sure they don't always see eye-to-eye, but look at all they've done as a team. The research, the books, the awards. They're legends in their field.

Here's what I'm going to present in my doc: two dedicated individuals working side by side for decades, loving what they do and loving each other; bound together by those two strong loves.

"And now, their love of discovery has led them to Raven," Keith continued. " 'Great Bird of Mystery'— that's my working title. Oh, I got some nice shots today. This may sound crazy coming from someone so well-grounded, but it's like he knew what was going on."

"Roy?"

"No, silly, the raven. Like he knew we were watching—and sensed our respect."

"That's a cartoon."

"Okay, yeah, I get imaginative when I'm absorbed in a project. You wouldn't understand that type of intense focus. You're too diffuse."

"And you wouldn't un—" Gloria stopped herself. After holding her breath for moment, she reverted to form. "Sorry, sorry. I guess I need to ease up a bit. Accept the situation for what it is. I mean, no one can make me feel one way or the other, right? My emotions are my responsibility. I know that, but sometimes..."

"I'm glad you've come to senses," Keith said. "Now, if you'll excuse me, I need to get some rest. Otherwise, I won't be able to keep up with that pair tomorrow. What powerhouses they are!" Keith rolled away from her in the sleeping bag. Gloria stared at his back for a few moments, then sighed in resignation and slumped down and curled into herself. She put a hand to her throat as if to protect herself—or soothe a hurt.

I waited until I heard both of them breathing comfortably in their sleep, then whispered my message —the Raven Dance instructions, the song—into her ear, then into his.

Then I hopped quietly over the other tent and put

that same incantation into the ears of Roy and Kay as they slept.

Afterwards, I stood by the glowing-red embers of the campfire, my heart racing in anticipation.

But to my chagrin, no one rose to do the dance. When I checked, I found Keith shifting peacefully in his slumbers. Gloria, meanwhile, stirred with agitation, as if fighting to wake while at the same time, fighting to stay asleep. My hopes rose, then collapsed as her struggle subsided with a sad-sounding sigh.

I didn't stay too long at the other tent: Roy grated my ears with his snoring. Kay merely gave an irritated murmur.

Yes, I was disappointed as I flew back to my roost. This project might take longer than expected.

The next day, I again posed at the cliff's edge in full view of the humans. Occasionally, I would give them a profile just to show a different aspect of myself. Or I'd flourish my wings and bow. Or I'd sidestep to right, then to the left, then to right again, then to left again. A little dance I hoped would amuse them—I thought they could use some amusement.

But despite my fun show, Keith gave the greater share of his attention to Kay and Roy. He trained his big shiny eye on them as they hiked through the wild grass toward my cliff. Gloria suffered in silence, trailing behind like a reluctant dog.

The reprieve of a night's sleep had not improved anyone's mood. All four seemed even more agitated today than the day before.

When the group finally reached the bottom of the cliff, I thought the time had come for me to make my move. First, I shook my tail feathers and head furiously as if bothered by mites. Then I raised my beak and cawed to the sky with an eruption had burned my throat.

As the humans watched and waited in wonder, I shot from the cliff's edge, swooped down over the valley, then angled back. As I flew over the four below, I blasted out another cry.

But I did not return to my perch. No, I disappeared down the gully of the mountain pass. For the time being, I would stay out of sight. I hoped to cause some distress in these people. Maybe the loss would shock them out of their heads. Maybe then they'd listen to their hearts. Maybe then they'd hear my song.

I didn't know what else to do.

I waited until late in the evening, then I made my way back to the campsite. Using the stealth common to our species, I crept into both tents and again whispered the incantation to all four sleepers.

Again, I waited by the glowing-red embers of the campfire. Again, no response.

So once again, I snuck into the tents; once again, I whispered the instructions.

But once again, my song failed rouse them. I was confounded. So much for my plan. Awake or asleep, these humans were blocked solid.

Desperate to solve my dilemma, I decided to linger longer than the night before.

Then, as I gazed into the dying red embers of the fire, I began to detect a jittery low-quality energy hanging around the campsite. Imagine a floating miasma, snapping with static. I'd felt that same angry tension before, during their campfire conversations. Residue, I assumed.

I was ready to fly from that disturbing buzz, when I saw the strangest sight: Roy walking about on stiff legs, his arms held straight out to the side as if hung with dried fish. But now his body was merely a shadow delineated by gray luminous lines. No physical substance, it seemed.

Then I spotted another such form nearby: Kay. Her shadow body stood stiff as oakwood, while her head moved slowly from side to side. But those blank eyes didn't seem to see anything. I'd seen that same look once on a dead bird—call it hollow-headed astonishment.

I stepped in front of her, just to test the situation. She didn't register my presence at all. Roy walked between us and kept going. The empty stare never left his eyes.

Strange, strange indeed.

Kay's spirit image intensified for a moment of brightness, then collapsed—vanishing into the dark.

Then I saw Keith hobbling along in a zigzag line, slumping to one side, with the shoulder on that side tilted and that knee bent, then slumping to the other side, with the other shoulder tilted and the other knee bent.

Gloria followed after him, her torso projecting forward and her arms outstretched, as if to catch the man, should he fall. Well that seemed to make sense—until she went right on past him, with her arms still out front. She was headed directly toward me. I decided to hold my place to see if she would stop. But no—her form slipped through me and she continued on. I merely felt a cool breeze permeate my being.

All through the night, the shadow forms of the four humans came and went—disappearing into the darkness, only to reappear moments later in another place. One time, Roy spread his arms out wide and opened his mouth as if singing a silent song. Another time, Kay laid down on the ground and clasped her knees to her chest. Later, I saw Keith slapping his face with one hand then the other. His eyes remained closed.

This scenario, taken as a whole, looked quite hideous. I now doubted if I could ever get through to all four humans. Unable to fulfill my duty, I might be stuck here forever. I'd gone through so much in my life and though I'd made mistakes, I had endured and benefited from my experiences. But these people might be my ruin. I felt nearly exhausted by frustration.

Fortunately, a few moments of beauty during that evening gave me hope.

Near dawn, Gloria's spirit form sat down cross-legged on the ground before me. No, she did not see me, but the listening in her blank blue eyes showed some awareness of my presence—she was listening to what she felt.

Prompted by this inner knowing, Gloria began to move her small lithe hands all around my raven body—not touching, but close enough for me to feel the soft energy radiating from her fingertips and palms—a gentle spirit, she was.

I believe she felt a summons from down deep in her being—a wordless voice telling her the healing of Raven waited, waited within. I could have touched her in that moment—we could have connected. But I knew I must hold back until everyone was ready: the humans had to do the dance together. We needed the power of a circle.

When the sunrise burned dusky red at horizon's edge, I flew away from the campsite. Not knowing what else to do, I would remain out of sight for another day.

After returning to the mountain cave I'd found the previous day, I worked my brain, trying to conceive an alternate plan. Oh, but I kept seeing those forms from the previous evening. Yes, their actions were clearly symbolic. But I need not interpret those symbols to know what they showed: not only were these humans not well, but their attempts to cure themselves actually made matters worse. "How depressing," I said to myself. Then I realized; at least they were trying. Well, another reason to hope.

But I needed more.

I tried to project myself to The Realm, but as usual when I felt so desperate, my efforts were useless.

My frustration now sank into depression. I began to cry "Help me help me help me" in my mind. I begged for Hak to reappear. I needed the calm of his voice. His equanimity.

I thought I could bear no more, but then I bore some more. Then around midday, to my surprise and relief, these feelings of despair began to ebb. Soon I felt empty as that cave. But now the lack of emotion seemed alright: at least this way, I'd survive the day.

I wondered if I should visit the campsite that night. I did not want a repeat of the previous evening. Yet I felt anxious—shouldn't I at least make another attempt?

To that question, a deep feeling answered "no". Did I dare trust this feeling? Did I dare do nothing at all? My logical mind said I should go. And yet, I couldn't seemed to pry my feet loose. So I hunkered down in the dripping cold of the cave and tried to rest.

The next day, I flew to the top of the cliff, but kept myself well-hidden as I watched the humans.

Around mid-morning, the group hiked out into the valley, scanning the sky as they made their way to the cliff wall.

When they reached the bottom of the cliff, they began picking their way through the scree and short pine along the side, then climbed through the boulders and rock toward the top.

The desperate worry on Roy's face had now softened into resignation. Oh the pain of watching that poor man realize his worst fear! Kay kept glaring at him, despising him for despising himself. Keith held his jaw muscles tight and his chin up. He refused to accept what he felt: the pervasive sense of weakness that comes when we believe we've failed.

As for Gloria, though she still slumped along, she was now the least unhappy of the lot. And why not?— she knew her ordeal might soon be over.

When they finally reached the cliff top, all knelt down on hands and knees and examined some footprints I'd left in the dust. Roy collected a few fallen feathers and even a little of my poop.

Then the four sat down to rest near the edge of the cliff. Keeping still as stone, I hid behind a clump of sagebrush and listened.

"Think he's chosen another roosting place?" Keith asked Roy. The two men gazed out over the valley.

"I hate to say that I think. But hey, maybe I'm wrong—there's still so much we don't know about Raven."

"Really? But they've been studied. I mean, everything's been studied."

"Yes, of course, but that doesn't mean we know everything."

"Everything? Or anything?" Kay took a puff from an invisible cigarette and blew pretend smoke into the air.

"You must study Raven at a distance, in order to truly know him. But distance also works against you."

"The king of irony speaks." Kay again puffed her

invisible cigarette and smiled with meanness.

"I'll tell you a little secret." Roy looked from Keith to Gloria then back to Keith in secretive way that seemed pretentious.   "I've long felt my work goes beyond research.   I'm searching, searching for a deeper understanding. Oh god, listen to me. It's this heat and the fact that I'm terribly frustrated and mad at myself. I feel like I let you down. Well, at least we got to see Raven—Raven in all his glory. I've never seen one strut so grandly. Quite a bird we lost."

Kay again puffed on her unseen cigarette.   Roy watched her with subtle sideways glances.

"Maybe it's good that some things evade our reach, our grasp—though when that happens I strain all the more," Roy continued with a chuckle. "I'm laughing but I'm bleeding. Oh, listen at me! The best scientists might be poets, but that doesn't mean they're good poets. I'm just rambling—stop me please. Accept my apologies. You two have been more than patient."

Looked as if my plan had failed—these four seemed ready to move on.   But who knows?—I'm planted the instructions, so they might still respond—if not now, later on. They could eventually go within and hear the song and then do the dance. In any case, I'd done the job. So perhaps I'd be allowed to return.

A reasonable thought—but one that felt false.

However, below the thought was that familiar feeling, the feeling that kept telling me: *all is as it should be.*   But because the feeling seemed so unreasonable, I still had doubts.

The shadows of late afternoon filled the campsite with a pool of darkness. The vacant, solitary faces of the humans looked downright funeral. Meal time was even more tense with unspoken anger. Afterwards, Roy doused the campfire with stale coffee and they all went to bed.

I thought I should visit their tents one more time—try one more time to call them to the dance. But once again, that deep feeling told me: *no, no, all will be okay.* So again, I rejected good sense and remained in the cave.

After breakfast the next morning, the four humans began to disassemble their camp. They collapsed their tents and heaved stakes from the ground. Though heavy with lethargy, they managed to stuff their equipment and provisions back into the wagon. The ghost of the campfire rose in a thin stream of smoke.

Yes, I felt anxious, watching them—though now, that feeling was so clear, so strong, wordlessly saying: *all is as should be, all will be okay.* I felt the impulse to do something—anything—but I knew I must sit and bide my time.

Finally, when the loading was nearly complete, I saw the shining light of opportunity. An opportunity that had shown itself before. But now I knew the time had come for me to act.

Roy had seemed so weary since rising that morning. But now, suddenly, he'd developed a little bounce to his step. Ever so often, he would glance over to the trees near the creek. Finally, he dropped the task at hand and, without a word to the others, began a swift walk toward those trees.

For reasons beyond me, these humans made their excretions into a ritual, worthy of specific locale. From previous observation, I knew that after Roy had made his offering at the designated shrine, he would walk over to the creek and wash his hands.

I was already waiting in hiding when he stooped to wash. I swooped down behind him and tapped his heel with my beak.

Roy sprang to his feet instantly and looked all about, then scanned the tall grass for any sign of movement. I knew he couldn't see me amid the dense growth.

Ever so gently, he began to creep through the grass, his breath bated, his lower lip dangling. Every couple of steps, he would pause and listen for my presence. But all he could hear was the blood drumming in his ears.

Roy's feet came so close I breathed a bit of the dust they stirred and had to sniffle a sneeze.

Then, as soon as he'd passed, I shot straight up, fluttered my wings loudly and settled down on the opposite side of the creek. Roy spun and froze in his tracks. He dared not take his eyes from me or make any sudden movement. His face, shadowed before, now glowed with light. His deepest desire created an aura around me. I was mystery to him and to him, mystery held the highest meaning. Mystery seemed to be a link to the world of greater depth he desired.

With quiet caution, he slid one foot toward the creek bank, then slid the other foot forward. In this patient manner, he edged toward the creek, without knowing what he'd do once he got there.

I did not move, I did not speak. I merely stared at Roy, drawing him with my dark eyes.

He stopped where the grass met the sloping bank. I could see he felt completely helpless as he gazed across the creek at me. He moved his lips, but did not dare disturb me with a sound. Finally, he knelt down and extended his hand. Yes, he realized the gesture was futile, but he didn't know what else to do.

I cawed at him then. Roy flinched, but held his position. I cawed at him again.

"Come here, come on over to me," I cawed at him.

And yes, he slowly rose from his knees and yes, he

did slip one foot down the sandy slope, then the other.

But then hesitated. I now sensed his fear of the water. He wanted me, but feared going into the deep pool between us. So I continued to caw, to urge him on, hoping that if he conquered his fear, a release would occur that would open him to my instruction.

But I needed to assure him that I wouldn't fly away if he attempted a crossing. So in a moment of inspiration, I tucked my wings in, stiffened my body and legs, then heaved myself over sideways and toppled to the ground. Lying there in a rigid pose, I felt a bit ridiculous.

Roy narrowed his eyes and studied me, unable to comprehend what had felled such a robust raven. He glanced back toward the campsite. He wanted to summon the others, but dared not leave me unguarded.

He skipped a pebble across the creek at me. But no, I did not stir. I kept my eyes open and blank. He tested the water with one finger. I then surprised him with a shriek and began to flap my free wing. By pushing against the ground with my talons, I managed to spin myself in circles, creating a picture of distress. I was the trickster indeed.

Roy stood back up. Watching the sliding water with dread, he pulled the shoes from his feet, then shed most of the clothes that covered his pudgy body. He had molted; he was ready for change.

Roy touched his big toe to the pool that swirled along the bank. Though the cold water sent a shock through his frame, our man remained strong in determination. Holding his breath, he walked into the creek until the water reached mid-thigh. In just those few steps, his face drained to a deathly pale. But still, he kept on. His body shook so hard that the water rippled around his hips.

Then with a step, he slipped and went all the way

under.

His head shot right back up, but only for moment. The head shot down again as if pulled by force.

Surface swirls appeared as Roy waved his arms and legs about beneath the dark green. The water began to churn and soon became a frothing white chaos. A fling of spray sparkled in the sun. Again, the head popped to the surface, gasping, spitting water, slinging its hair about wildly. Then again, went under—and this time, stayed under.

Suddenly all became still. I peered into the dim green water to see Roy's body just hanging there, its arms dangling listlessly. Hair drifted above the head in a wispy mess.

Released of its tension, the bloated body soon floated to the surface, face down, and began to go with the current. I followed along.

After a short distance, the body hit a large rock, twirled around, and lodged under some brush drooping from the bank.

Fortunately, I then spied Kay striding through the tall grass. She'd just completed her own visit to the shrine.

I leapt into the air, flapped my wings, and cried to her. When she spotted me, the anger suddenly left her face, replaced by the light of happy surprise. I glided in small circles over the creek near Roy's body. She began walking my way, slowly, cautiously, watching me closely. I dropped to the bank and went into my act again— flapping, kicking, shrieking. But the moment Kay extended her arm, I dove into the hanging brush. She then got down on one knee and peered into the tangle. Seeing Roy's body, she stood up abruptly.

She glanced once in the direction of camp, then quickly removed her shoes and stepped into the water. Holding the carcass by the hands, she pulled it to shore.

Then with a couple of sharp tugs, managed to land it on the bank. Roy's face slapped down sideways on a flat rock.

Kay first put her head on his chest, then she held her fingertips to a wrist. Unable to find any life, she stood again in that old arms-akimbo stance. At first, her face wore a mask of numb shock. But as she continued to stare at the limp, lumpy dumb body, her anger began to return—Roy had gotten the last word, hadn't he? That dead walrus body represented all she'd ever despised about him. She could never provoke any real fire from the man. When she challenged him, he always played the all-suffering victim, patiently taking her abuse as if trying to irritate her even more. What a manipulator!

She felt like speaking her mind one last time, but chastising a dead man seemed foolish. She laughed at herself then, and experienced an odd sense of release.

After she'd wiped the tears of laughter away, her curiosity rose. Death lay right at her feet. Kay knelt again. She started to touch a shoulder she'd touched many times before. But that shoulder seemed so different now. She stood again, then after musing for a moment, put a foot on the thick bicep and gave it a wiggle. Such a strange feeling. Taken out of her usual mode of thought, she began to play with that piece of cold fat, rolling it back and forth with the ball of her foot. The hand showed palm, then back, then palm again, then back.

Kay took her toes off the bicep and regarded the body of her companion again. After a moment, she lifted her leg backward, held the foot for a beat, then let go with a sharp kick to the ribs that shook Roy's entire frame. The blubbery lips, pressed sideways into the rock, let out a gurgling sound.

Kay froze in an instant, then went to her knees,

heaved the man over and listened for a heartbeat again. She waited several moments, then finally gave up and lifted her head from the chest. Only then did she notice the bulging eyeballs staring at her with the blank astonishment of death.

At last, the reality of the situation hit her fully. Kay covered her face and began to weep.

After Roy lost consciousness, his body had loosened its grip on the spirit-self and that spirit-self had drifted free. For a few moments, it'd floated closely overhead, uncertain of its status. Then it spotted the pale body below. But before it could go back, I blocked its path and began to whisper the incantation. The song held it fast.

When I had finished, I released the spirit-self and it dove down. Roy's body took it back in like a whirlpool sucking down a twig.

When Kay heard the sputtering, she uncovered her face. Water streamed from Roy's mouth; his chest heaved with breathing. She felt surprise, then wonder, then relief.

Then a massive wave of guilt.

She knelt again and whispered in Roy's ear with a new sweetness, "Roy darling? Papa Bear? Can you hear me? Are you...are you alright? No, don't move. Just lie still. I was sure you were...how you could still be...Well, never mind. You just take it easy now. I was so scared!"

Roy heard her, but just barely—dazed as he was in the blissful afterglow of Raven wisdom song. His lids hung halfway down his eyeballs and he wore a crumpled, drunken smile. To calm her nervous voice, he mumbled, "I'm okay, honey. Don't worry. Everything's fine. Really. Just fine. Fine. Downright froggin' wonderful, in fact. Yes, yes, it is. Yes."

Roy saw a corona of blue and gold fuzzing around Kay's face. He felt her guilt and wanted to comfort her. But didn't have the words. He lifted his hand to touch her arm, but that seemed wrong somehow, so he set it back down. During the tedious grind of the last few years, he'd often wondered if he actually loved the woman. Now he felt his love again, but also understood their dance together was done. A painful realization. But he felt happy for Kay. Away from him, she would be a better person. She'd be released from the hard toil of pounding him down—a job that brought her so much secret shame.

Roy wanted to rise from the bank, but knew Kay would force him to recuperate. So he said, "Honey, know what I'd really like right now? Some saltines, that's what. Would you mind getting them for me? We still have half a box, I think."

"Saltines?" she said, confused.

"Yeah, it's weird, but I have a sudden craving for a cracker right now. Just a square or two would probably be enough. Set me right, it would."

"Don't you think you should wait?" Kay said softly. "I mean, you almost...I don't understand—you've always been so afraid of the water. Were you trying to...no, no, no, of course not, no. It was just an accident, I'm sure."

"Please, a saltine."

Kay stood up, but hesitated. She examined Roy's face. He seemed so relaxed—those were the heavy lids of a man resting in richest luxury. Even so, she felt unsure.

"Don't worry, I'm not delirious," he murmured.

Well, what could she do? After one last look, Kay ran for the campsite.

Roy patted the sandy bank affectionately, then with a deep breath, lifted himself up. Once he'd found his clothes, he stole away into the dense grove.

Of course, he didn't really want a cracker. He just needed a few solitary moments in which to savor this quiet ecstasy before he rejoined the others. He knew his life had changed somehow. Perhaps he'd had one of those near-death experiences. Yes, yes—he now recalled gazing down at his body. But the song I'd sung to him was not in his memory. In its place, he remembered gliding through a tunnel toward a black silhouette surrounded by white light—a silhouette he recognized as Raven. Towering, intimidating. Yet also seen as "sanctuary", as home.

But before the event could climax, I'd ended my song and the vision had popped in his head like a bubble.

Yes, must've been a near-death experience, he decided. In any case, he knew he couldn't return to his old ways. What his new life would be, Roy couldn't imagine. But for now, he just wanted to move through this island of trees and feel sunlight and shadow flow over his body. He wanted to burn his nose with the scent of dusty sagebrush. He wanted to roll around in the harsh sun-burnt grass until his skin roared with the feeling. In short, he wanted to spread his senses as far and as deep as possible.

Kay was close to horrified when she returned to find Roy gone. She started to call out his name, but stopped. She realized the man had tricked her—and in a flash of intuition, understood why. Yes, he'd needed a break, but more than that: his near-death had created a change in him. And not just for this one day. This change would change their relationship. She knew they would no longer be together.

Kay slunk away through the tall grass until she found a small clear space. There, she collapsed on the ground, curled herself up, and began to cry. She wanted to cry all of the guilt out, guilt over her constant cruel behavior. She took the anger she usually focused on Roy and turned it on herself. She clawed her skin and dug her head into the point of a stone. I wanted to connect then, to link her spirit-self to mine, but knew the time had not yet come.

After awhile, Kay feared she might not be able to shut this flood of feeling back down. She felt stings of pain all over her body. *I've just got too many demons,* she thought. *I'm too far gone to ever get right again.*

Hoping for release, she uncurled herself and with arms and legs out, she shouted aloud, "Demons be gone!"—and in so saying, suddenly felt silly.

But to her surprise—and relief—that moment of foolishness seemed to calm the storm. Yes, she knew the storm still lived within her, just beneath the surface. And knew in time it would rise again and once again, she'd be overwhelmed. But for now, she would enjoy the peace she'd created for herself, enjoy this temporary reprieve.

As Kay closed her eyes and settled in, another odd but pleasant feeling crept into her frame: the force within her—the energy that bound her together—seemed to relax its hold. Her first response was to clamp down. But she found she just didn't care. *Ah let it go,* she thought.

A peculiar sensation filled her body—a soft pervasive vibration. She imagined the particles of her being loosening, moving apart, drifting like space dust through an inner emptiness. She marveled at this sensation and wanted to ride the feeling out—to see how long she could maintain that delicate balance. So she kept absolutely still, despite a giddy feeling of uncertainty.

That's when her spirit-self, sensing my presence, managed to slip free and come to me as I hovered overhead. As before, I sang my instructions. But all Kay recalled was an abrupt shift that shot her down a tunnel toward the silhouette of Raven: a form towering and intimidating, but also seen as "sanctuary", as home.

But right before climax, I ended the song and directed the spirit-self back down. I'd prepared Kay for the dance.

When she suddenly came back to herself, Kay thought, *Must've been a dream. Yes, I guess I drifted off—that'd explain those odd sensations in my body.*

In any case, she felt wonderful—a flower had opened and she was the child in the cradle of its fresh spring bloom. A sense of beauty now overwhelmed her. What she saw and heard, she also felt within: the dead leaves crunching beneath her feet, a spider web swinging in the crook of a tree, a snake peeking from beneath a rock. She wanted to go to Roy. She had so many things to tell him—she wanted to tell him she loved him. Yes, to her own surprise, she now realized she loved him. Yet at the same time, she also understood that now it was too late to make amends—but for some reason, that was okay.

And so she allowed herself to walk in wonder, luxuriating as the long grass brushed her legs.

I knew Keith was next. Scanning the land below with my sharp raven eyes, I found him sitting in a place where two willow trees swept the ground and a long line of ants carried pieces of leaves to a secret destination.

The man was all hunched up, his pointy knees nearly pinned to his chin. He told himself he needed these stolen moments to help unfasten his mind, to give nascent ideas freedom to develop. But he felt guilty because he had not accomplished this unfastening on his own. No, he'd enlisted the aid of the plant kingdom. Nothing wrong with that really, except that he had sought this aid more and more often of late. But increased use had not increased the light. Quite the opposite. He now questioned his powers of thought, questioned his ability to see and to create. Doubt had a hook-hold on his mind. *I'm just dead inside my head,* he told himself. *Before when I indulged, I could watch dust motes in the afternoon light and imagine a new world in each one. But now...now I just see dull dirt. And yet, I don't quit—why? I guess because I feel even more empty the other way.*

Keith fell back into the fallen leaves, flinging his arms and legs out wide and closing his eyes on the world. Those ants ran in a steady stream beside his head.

His mind and body, in this weakened state, rested in the twilight land between waking and sleep, and so, had only a tenuous grip on his spirit-self. That spirit-self could feel my presence and given this opportunity, slipped free quite easily and glided up to me.

As I whispered the incantation, Keith suddenly found himself traveling down a tunnel toward Raven. Contrary to my expectation, he did not resist—he was quite willing to lose himself, quite willing to surrender.

Of course, I ended the song before the moment of climax and spun his spirit-self back down. But this time, I acted a bit too abruptly—his body went into a seismic fit as the spirit reentered. However, by fighting to settle himself, Keith actually regained some of his gumption.

Then, as he blinked his eyes open, he suddenly noticed the leaves above him—how they splintered sunlight into prisms.

He mused for a moment on his Raven dream, then shrugged and stood up, arrow-straight and true.

With a full circle rotation, he surveyed the surrounding environment; he drank it all in and breathed it all out. Suddenly everything seemed to him to be what he'd always said it was—that is, equally sacred. The dirt as well as the clouds.

In this new mode of being, Keith knew his fear and confidence simultaneously and felt both humble and strong.

"I am done here," he said aloud without thinking.

But no, that wasn't quite right.

Allowing Keith this time to appreciate the sanctity of the commonplace, I took flight.

For the first time in days, Gloria found herself alone at the campsite. *What a strange feeling,* she said to herself. First, Roy had gone off on some unknown errand. Then Kay had left, only to rampage back, in a frantic search for some saltine crackers. As a substitute, Gloria had given her a little box of animal cracker snacks. Kay then hurried off without offering any explanation. Amid this confusion, Keith had done another one of his disappearing acts.

But to her surprise, Gloria did not feel relieved by this new solitude. The entire trip, she'd felt like a hostage, bound to two prisoners who were their own jailers. Keith by himself had long been headache enough. She'd once believed she could learn from him. He'd seemed expansive and aware. But now she saw him as narrow and isolated: afraid of any idea that might challenge his beliefs. She tried to be careful, but sometimes *she just had to say something.* Then when her words came out in a burst, that something was often something she regretted saying.

And so, when Keith *strongly suggested* she should go on this trip, Gloria had groaned inside with a big "No!". Yet, to her surprise, she found herself giving an immediate "Yes".

"Why'd I do this to myself?" she asked the wind.

But she knew why. The one she called "The Little Demon" had tricked her again. There seemed to be something within that kept pushing her to go where she didn't want to be. Was she trying to punish herself, spurred by some deeply-buried guilt? Or was the Little Demon taking her up the hard road, so that she might become a better person? She hoped so—she hoped there was a higher purpose behind the bumps and lumps of this road.

Gloria paced around the dead campfire, looking for that higher purpose in the events of the last few days. But only one intuition came to her, hard to accept but undeniable: they were not yet done here.

A cool rush of wind shot right through her. Low black clouds began to move in. Gloria now saw the campsite as a war-torn area: abused and strangely vacant. The whole place seemed inhabited by a ghostly malaise—the psychic debris of their occupancy. She had to escape.

I knew a thread connected the two of us. That thread would guide her to me—I need not pull. So I waited as Gloria walked out through the tall grass, then down into the valley, then up the ridge to the top of the cliff.

She felt as if the low streaming clouds might scrape the hair off her head. Gazing out over the wind-swept valley and lake, she could feel a power tremoring within —as if some unknown something might suddenly burst forth.

Feeling the need for release, she raised her arms and let out a scream that rode with the wind out over the valley. Then she looked all about, frantically searching for something—anything—to grasp and hold to herself. Her eyes were wide, wild, and luminous blue.

I knew the time had arrived. So I presented myself to her—I stood directly before her in my physical form. She grew completely still, held by the wonder of seeing Raven. Slowly, she knelt down. I bowed to her then and I began my silent communique: what I knew to be true in regards to her. Unfortunately, I can only express the message here using clumsy words:

"I know you felt my presence the other day at dawn. I realized then you were more open than the other three. But I waited before making the connection, because what must be done is best done with the four of you together—the power of four heightens the experience.

"The others have opened now—opened to a transformation they fear yet desire with all their hearts. Fear because it feels like death, yet desire, because it's a resurrection.

"Yes, your life will change for the better, but that doesn't mean it'll be easier. No, more difficult—you're really going to have a time of it, from here on out. You'll endure ridicule on a regular basis. Blunt-headed folk will shout you down and insult you. But you'll never play the victim again. You've already performed that role to perfection. *It is time for you to move on.*"

I then focused my intent directly on her heart. Unlike the other three, she didn't need to leave her physical form. The information flowed directly to her. She accepted the song—she acquiesced and felt the power of submitting to her own deep will.

What a relief to be done with the hard part of my job! This trial had forced me to dig a little deeper down into my own Raven well. I felt ready for the final act.

I now placed myself at the apex of the sky: I was the

center—the fulcrum for this event. The humans met on the plain below, one at each of the four points. They bowed to one another.

I then began to spin, twining the invisible threads that ran from me to them; in this way, bringing the four humans together in the center of the circle.

Then I spun in the opposite direction, separating the threads and in that way, spreading the people back out again. And so the dance went—with me spinning in one direction, then the other, and the humans, in response, joining together in the center, then stepping back, back to the four points. By following their higher will, the four found freedom in submission.

Though I led, I was not the controller—just the empty hub where all spokes met. Not so bad being nothing—a relief, not being me.

As they moved over the horizontal plane of that flat ground, the humans also moved vertically—they deepened down into their depths. In a long short time, they found Raven down there—that wisdom. Raven then lifted them out and up, up to the sky.

The dance ended when, after another long short time, the group returned, returned to being Roy, Kay, Keith, and Gloria—the same people, but different; forever after, different.

At that point, I was no longer needed and so, fell away naturally like a husk—free as a dead leaf spinning down. Even less than nothing.

After I don't know how long, I woke to find myself hovering in a black space. I had slipped back, back into my usual way of being, my usual mindset. And so, I began to feel my usual uncertainty. During the dance I was free of thought; I had no doubts. Ah, what a luxury!

"Well, at least now I can return to Allo and the brood," I thought. "No one has said differently, so it must be okay."

But how to find my way back? In this darkness, I found no stars to guide me, no moon. I could see no landmarks. Hoping for some instruction from Hak, I tried to project myself to The Realm. But that's nearly impossible to do with your wings moving and your anxiety rising.

"I need some solid ground under my feet," I said to myself. "Maybe I should just rest for the night."

So I angled my wings and began to descend. Such an uncomfortable feeling, not being able to see the land below. I kept waiting to touch down, but no—there seemed to be no bottom to this darkness.

In any case, I didn't really want to wait 'til morning —I was desperate to return. So I pulled myself back up a bit and leveled my flight out, hoping I wouldn't slam into some cliff hidden in the darkness. "I should be okay," I said to myself. "I'm protected by the higher will within, right? I'm guided by the higher will within, right?"

I thought I saw the flash of a falling star far in distance. "That must be a sign," I thought. "I must be headed in the right direction."

But as I forced myself forward, the dry air harshed in my lungs. My strength began to ebb, but I only pushed harder. "No amount of pain can match the love in my heart," I said to myself. "I will gladly sacrifice my body, in order to reach my family."

Suddenly my skin prickled with an odd sensation. Strange, strange—I could feel the quill tips loosening in my flesh. Feathers began slipping from my back and wings and popping from my tail. Soon, my hide stung all over. Naked, I was. But no matter—I just figured it was my time to molt. When I arrived home, I would be a new bird, both inside and out.

But then, even stranger sensations: I could feel my skin drooping, and then drop in dollops from my frame. Strips of flesh and muscle flew off my limbs like leaves ripped from a tree by a hard wind. Cold air blew all around my heart. One by one, organs fell down through the spaces of my bare skeleton. And yet, driven by my desire to return, I refused to stop. "This can't be happening," I told myself. "I'm sure I'll be okay."

Then the bones of my skeleton unhinged. In glimmers of white, they drifted down and away through the night. But still, I did not stop—I maintained focus and kept striving forward. "All will be fine once I arrive home."

However, now I couldn't tell if I was making progress or not. I could no longer feel my wings moving. I could no longer feel the air rushing over my body. I'd left my physical body before, but my physical body had never left me. For that matter, I wasn't even sure if I had the substance of a spirit body. If I didn't, then what was I? A soul? We sometimes spoke of the soul, but what was it exactly?

I then deepened my concentration, hoping to determine the nature of my being. I seemed to be no more than a mere speck, a grain of sand. I began to feel the enormity of the Universe pressing against me on all sides—and growing ever more intense. I was a virus. In an effort to preserve my tiny self, I curled within— became a hard knot—which only seemed to intensify the force. I'd surely burst—I'd break—and then what? —my dust would disperse in all directions through infinite space.

"But I don't want to be everywhere!" I cried. "I want to go home!"

Well...I must've blacked out from the excruciating

pain. In any case, I next remember popping up as a weed in a morning prairie. The red-tinted sky of dawn shone above me. Pink frost sparkled on smooth stones.

"Well, at least, I'm rooted down," I thought to myself.

But I had little time to rest: events happened so fast in this new place. Spurred by an unnameable desire, my weed-self shot straight up until it merged with a red cloud in that red sky. The rise felt heady, felt thrilling, but the red fog roiled around me restlessly and my thin stalk wavered in the wind and my roots seemed to loosen in the earth.

But as the cloud began to thin, I felt the warmth of my heart opening and looked to find a girl-child in the basket formed by my yellow petals. Though I wanted to shelter her, she stood up and abruptly leapt down and spun down and down, and landed softly far below—by the time she touched down, she was a full-grown woman.

As a woman, she plucked a needle from a cactus and ran away across the plain to mend the tattered horizon.

I wanted to go with her, but knew she didn't need whatever I could give her.

As a tear fell from my sagging flower, the sun died behind a storm cloud and the land grew dark. In the far distance, I could see a black wave riding across the land —its crest rising straight up in front, a crest nearly high as the clouds.

This wave swept up all in its path and its path seemed to be aimed toward the thin wavering weed I was.

As I watched helplessly, the wave rolled right up to my stalk. It reined to halt with the flip of its crest teetering perilously above my weed-head. In the shock of fright, my stalk shot back down and my flower folded into a bulb that burst on the ground and I bounded forth from its broken shell as a man—an anxious man who ran across the plain with his strong limbs pumping as the dark wave roared after him—sometimes so close, drops of water struck my back. I ran into the hills without once stopping.   I attacked the highest mountain.

Scrambling up that jumble of stone, working my arms and legs with angry speed, in short time I reached the tippy-top of the peak, where I found a lone pine tree. The wave was now a river snaking its way up—a long rush of water switching back and forth through gray piles of rock.

What could I do but dig my human fingers into the pine tree bark and propel myself up by pushing against the trunk with my heels. Driven by a furious ferocity, I'd soon hoisted myself all the way up to the highest limb. But oh, that damn wave slipped right on up the trunk, determined to do me in.

But bad fortune can bring good—I then spied a hole in the sky just above me. Like a frog I leapt and in a moment of perfection, shot through that circle.

I covered the opening with a big wet eyeball, then turned to find a group of beings with raven heads and the bodies of men surrounding me on this wide field of blue. They grabbed my arms and legs and hoisted me high in celebration—they tossed me up one time, two times, three times—four!

Then they set me back down and recited their story to me, speaking as one, their voices blending and becoming the low song of a river, patient and relentless.

This river told how the raven-men had once lived on earth, but driven by the pain of life, they'd struggled to gain perspective and in that way, eventually lifted themselves up. So now they lived in the clouds— sometimes descending to help humans when the big eyeball spotted someone in trouble and began to weep.

Filled with appreciation for them, I blinked away sweet tears.

But then these keepers laid me down and held me down and began to pierce my tender flesh with their black beaks—each spike, a new fire; my whole body screamed from the shock of so much sudden pain.

The raven-men knocked a window in my skull, ripped away my throat, then punctured my bladder. They tore out my intestines in spiraling ribbons. And on and on until, at the end of their mayhem, I was no more than a single wet ribbon with just enough strength to slink away like a worm. This group of beings then vanished into white mist. Rather than stay here, I decided to risk the earth realm again.

Fortunately, I was thin enough to squeeze past the eyeball in the hole. To my relief, the wave had disappeared. So I slid down the pine tree, then slipped down the mountain, down through the hills, then moved across the prairie desert in little leaps until I reached the place where I'd once been a weed. I'd returned hoping that my daughter might have returned. But no. So, I decided I best seek sanctuary and eased myself down the old weed hole, which I discovered, led to a dark tunnel.

The tunnel went this way and that, then back again and finally ended in a cavernous room. On that cold gray floor, I found my pathetic worm-self surrounded by women with raven heads and human bodies.

They stepped slowly in a circle, moving one way with heads bent down, then turning to go in the opposite way with heads uplifted, then reversing track again and lowering their heads. Their murmuring chant, echoing off the walls, told how they'd fled to this world long ago to escape a drought; told how they fed on rich minerals that grew here; told how they'd found an underground river in which to cleanse themselves.

As they recited their story, I felt the deep quiet strength of this place move into the small scrap of tissue that I was. Soon, I felt the odd jerks and jumps of bone and muscle abruptly gaining bulk. Feather nubs popped up in black buds on glistening white flesh.

A few magical moments later, I stood up fresh—a new version of my old raven self.

The raven-women then converged on me in celebration. They tossed me up, up into the air. One time, two times, three times—four!

Then they said that I must go—the cave river would lead me home. I begged them to let me stay—I wanted to live in their healing world forever. But they grabbed me by the wings and feet, then heaved me into the river and turned away.

I flapped and floundered in the water for a bit, but soon accepted and settled and let the current pull me along. I then dreamt a dream that told me everything about everything, which I then forgot when I woke to find myself again on a sun-scorched desert.

I saw, a short distance away, a skeleton tree black with ravens. I cawed to them, but their ears did not seem to hear me, their eyes did not seem to see me. "My brothers, my sisters," I cried, "do you not know me?"

Then as one, the birds struck up into the sky and I stood alone again. Bright vaporous light obscured the horizon on all four sides. A big blue snake suddenly became a blue stream. Happily, I dunked my head under the water. A black clam resting on the riverbed opened up, then clamped shut, opened up, then clamped shut. Again and again, the clam opened, then clamped shut. The white shine of its pearl blinked on and off, on and off.

Abruptly a force drew me backward, out of the water. I found a rope tied to my leg. This rope stretched to the hand of man covered with autumn leaves and twigs. He trudged through the sand, dragging me along behind. When I tried to take flight, he didn't even glance back, but brought me down to the ground with one yank of his rope. I pecked at the knot, but that fist only tightened its grip.

At the skeleton tree, the autumn man looped the rope over a branch, then cinched it up tight. I swung in the air, strung upside down. "At least now I can rest," I said. "At least now I can rest."

After a long time or a short time, I awoke at the abandoned campsite of the four humans. A spinning wind twirled gray ash up from their dead campfire. Wagon tracks pointed due west. I said a silent thanks to those humans—they'd served me well.

Then I again took flight—again, with the intention of going home. But this time, I would not try to force my way—I would be patient and allow the wind to take me there if there was where I needed to be. If not, I'd accept being elsewhere. Yes, I'd learned that lesson before. But it's easy to forget, especially when you're in distress.

Even if my way did lead me back to the flock, I wouldn't return to my former life. I now knew I could do more and so, I must—to do less would only create problems. The previous shaman had actually been right: I could not stay where I was—in terms of responsibility.

The mountain peaks below me gradually smoothed into graceful hills. Small pine trees replaced sagebrush. Then the taller pine replaced the small, only to be usurped by broad leafy trees.

Then those familiar redwoods rose again. Soon, I

spotted the clearing the flock used as its gathering place.

I dropped down through the trees and settled on a steepled boulder. In short time, Kreck arrived.

That plain, solid bird studied me for a few moments. He cocked his head and squinced up one eye. Kreck could see that something strange had happened to me. But also sensed that the event was beyond his comprehension. In any case, he understood, as I did, the real reason behind my return.

"I hope you've stopped deceiving yourself?" More a statement than a question.

"What about the other shaman?"

"Dropped dead just yesterday."

"Maybe he knew I was coming back."

"No, don't think so. Said he didn't like being a raven. Told me he wanted to try life as a coyote."

"He won't like it," I said.

"Well, I'm relieved he's gone."

"He lost favor?" I dreaded to hear the story. I hoped the flock wouldn't blame me.

"Let's just say he wasn't a true shaman," Kreck shook his head. "Anyone can perform a ritual. Anyone can tell us to follow our own intuition. Which of course, we should do.

"But sometimes we need someone who'll tell us what we already know deep within but won't admit to ourselves. We need someone connected to his own depths, so that he knows what we know deep within. Someone not too proud, but proud enough to try to be the best version of himself. Maybe you think you don't fit description and maybe it doesn't quite fit yet. But I think it will, and soon enough. In the meantime, it probably fits you better than it does many who've long called themselves 'shaman'.

"You have a certain presence—we all recognize

171

that.   This presence, it comes from the power of experience—not just what one has endured, but what one has learned from what one has endured. You think you haven't learned much, but that tells me you'll keep trying to learn because you know you don't know everything.

"I realize you may still reject the position. Well, okay, but in that case, to be honest, we don't really need you."

"I realize now why I was afraid of the job.   I believed it to be a burden I lacked the strength to bear. I knew I was wounded and thought, ideally, a shaman should be someone who's healed his wounds. But no— now I see that process of healing is never complete. The fools I've met are those who believe they're alright —believe they know everything. At least, I know better than that. I know I must keep working, keep healing, keep learning. And in that way, I'll learn how to help others. And become strong enough to do the job as it needs to be done."

To my surprise, four seasons had passed during my absence—hard to track time when you're living a story of a death and rebirth. Guided by her intuition, Allo had recently chosen another mate. This new beau of hers had spindly legs, a stubby beak, and spent much time watching dust motes drift through angles of light. But I trusted Allo's judgment, knowing she'd followed her higher instinct.

As for our brood...

I was no more than a distant memory to them. Since my departure, their environment had bombarded them with all sorts of stimuli. They'd hardly had time to reflect on what they'd lost. "Probably for the best," I told myself—though I did feel a bit hurt. Maybe they'd eventually think back on their beginnings and seek out my company. But for the time being, I would have to appreciate them from a distance.

Our son Tok, cautious and ponderous from the start, had gained a sharper edge through training for the hunt. Kreck and Brok now advised him on the ways of leadership. Someday, Tok and his mate would take their place.

Our other son, Kra, had managed to focus his wild energy. He now explored the things of this earth more carefully, driven by a desire for deeper understanding. By learning to follow his inner promptings, no matter how bizarre they might seem, he would guide others to new ways of seeing.

Our daughter Ga now spent most of her time tending to herself, waiting for the right mate. The vicissitudes of growth had transformed her body into an awkward contraption. Her legs looked a little too short and her feet, a little too big. Her tail feathers crossed at odd angles and one wing hitched up higher than the other. Allo was helping her cope with this frustrating development, teaching her that true grace comes from within. Devoid of any unusual ambitions, Ga was fortunate that life had given her this problem to surmount.

The only one missing was our other daughter, Pruk —my favorite—the feisty runt. Shortly after my departure, illness had spun her into an extended delirium. She'd emerged from that feverish fight exuding a peculiar energy. For awhile, Kreck believed she might be the one to succeed the yes-no shaman. But the Master Raven had directed her elsewhere— she'd left the flock. I knew she'd be wounded many times in many ways, during her travels—often the wound coming from her own foolish behavior. As with the father, so with the daughter.

But in this way, she would learn, she would grow as she worked to heal her wounds.

A long time has now passed since my return. I never saw Pruk again—except in my dreams. But life follows laws of compensation, doesn't it? Here you are, seeking to learn from me what she would have sought to learn. Your path has led you here, just as my path once led me here. When I assumed the position of shaman, I hardly knew the trappings of the trade, the mumbo jumbo: the procedures that create a space where healing can occur. But really, that's easy enough to pick up. You've already done the hard part.

Hopefully, this tale, this story of the life given to me to live, will help you as you work to understand your own story—maybe make that story a little easier to accept, to digest.

Yes, I believe my story can be good medicine. Speaking for myself, I've just heard it for the umpteenth time and as before, I feel better afterwards.

But perhaps that was due to your presence, your thoughtful patient listening, dear shaman, hungry sprout.

Now, my tale is complete, and soon, soon, my life will also be.

###

end note:

In 1995, when I wrote this book I wasn't familiar with the term "cultural appropriation". But I realize some may still criticize me, saying that I used something that didn't belong to me. I reject that idea, for a couple of reasons, which I won't go into here. But I will say: I feel as if the tales that appear in this book appropriated me. These trickster tales tricked me into telling them again! Often tales can trick us in this way, but the ones of my own tribe—those of the Celtic tradition—didn't draw me in.

Anyway, if I have sinned, I've paid dearly for that sin. The process of writing and rewriting and rewriting this book was grueling (no hyperbole, there). As for the process of finding a publisher back in 1996, simply stated: it was humiliating and frustrating. As was the process of promoting the book once it was published. My net gain? I'm still in the red, I assure you.

Yes, all along the way, I've been humbled—which happens to be a key theme in the book. So whether or not these stories belong to me, they apparently tell my story. And not just mine, I believe, but ours.

ready to stop a cannonball
with his bare hand

also by Michael R. Patton

POETRY
My War for Peace
Searching for My Best Beliefs
Common Courage: poems of our story
Butterfly Soul: poems of death & grief & joy
Glorious Tedious Transformation: poems of change
Myth Steps: searching for the new mythology
Listening to Silence: poems of meditation
Survival: documenting the fight
What I Learned While Alone
The Truth of the Dream
Poet, Heal Thyself
finding Beauty

NOVELS
Dancing to Raven's Song
Soultime

STORIES
40 New Fables

NONFICTION
I'm Responsible:
a pessimistic optimist responds
to the trouble of his time

for more poetry:
    http://skyrope.wordpress.com
to hear these poems read aloud:
    https://soundcloud.com/mythsteps
searching for the new mythology:
    http://mythsteps.wordpress.com
my bloneironic:
    http://dreamsteps.wordpress.com
find "Michael R. Patton poetry"on YouTube

for discussions, dissensions & praises:
    livingbell@yahoo.com